OUR LADY OF THE SIGN

ABIGAIL FAVALE

Our Lady of the Sign

A Novel

IGNATIUS PRESS   SAN FRANCISCO

The characters and events in this book are fictional, and any resemblance to actual persons or events is coincidental.

Quotations from Sylvia Plath, "Metaphors", are quoted from *The Collected Poems*, ed. Ted Hughes (Harper Perennial, 1992).

Quotation from T.S. Eliot, "The Waste Land", is quoted from *The Waste Land and Other Poems* (Vintage Books, 2021).

Cover art:
Photograph of hallway by Filip Kominik, Unsplash.com

Detail of Mother of God of Tenderness Towards Evil Hearts by Kuzma Petrov-Vodkin, 1914. Public domain image

Cover design and photo illustration by John Herreid

© 2025 by Ignatius Press, San Francisco
All rights reserved
ISBN 978-1-62164-682-2 (PB)
ISBN 978-1-64229-299-2 (eBook)
Library of Congress Control Number 2025934380
Printed in the United States of America ∞

For Lindsay

There are two ways, one of life and one of death, and there is a great difference between the two ways.

— *The Didache*

There appeared to him that object which he had often seen before, but had never understood. It seemed to be something most beautiful, and, as it were, gleaming with many eyes.

— *The Autobiography of St. Ignatius*

I have unearthed your great wound; this bloom on your side is destroying you.

—Franz Kafka, "A Country Doctor"

One

"I need a writing holiday," she tells him, which is a lie. "I need to lock myself in a snowed-in cabin and finish this article. I have a deadline." This is also a lie, the part about the deadline, but Peter doesn't ask any questions, voice any doubts. The world of academe is, to him, a bizarre alternate reality with its own rhythm and rules that he feels no compunction to learn. He is a tradesman, a woodworker—a career choice that has proved to be auspicious in the frenzied housing boom, custom homes cropping up all over, built-in shelving and hand-distressed hardwood floors galore. Peter always seems to have a backlog of work requests, his prime pick of projects. Meanwhile, academia is a sinking ship on fire, and Simone is begging once-prestigious, now-readerless journals to publish the dissertation she has stripped for parts. She feels like a supplicant vying for a deathbed blessing from a rich uncle whose last pleasure in life is exercising the power to say no.

Peter likes poetry; they share that common love, but any mention of *theory* or *-isms* or *discourse* and his eyes will glaze over and he'll reach across to grab the mandolin he made but doesn't know how to play, idly testing the strings, nodding but no longer listening.

He doesn't seem to mind when she announces this plan for a writing holiday, which means that she'll be spending much of her three-week winter break in a different state and that he'll be spending Christmas and New Year's alone. She is both relieved and offended at this nonchalance. Relieved that he didn't ask "Which article?" or

"When's the deadline?"—yet offended that he didn't attempt to talk her out of it, to persuade her to spend the break with him. It wouldn't have worked, but she would have liked him to try.

The urge to leave had come to her after a conversation with her mother several days ago. It was a Saturday, and Simone was whirring around her townhouse, tidying corners and nooks that no human eye had ever seen, scrubbing them with a rag, her dark hair falling in her face in damp whisps. Her mind kept pulling toward a particular question like a dog that had caught the scent of a rank, hidden animal, but she kept the leash taut. She was not ready to face that question yet. She needed more time. She needed to keep busy.

When the phone rang, she answered it quickly, reflexively, welcoming any possible distraction. It was her mother, Cynthia, calling as she did every month, to have a conversation that would last about twenty minutes and follow the usual contours: First, Simone would be greeted by an account of the latest distant relative or past acquaintance who had died—"Do you remember X?" she'd ask, which was always a death knell. Then would follow a rundown of either her health, if it had been poor, or a recommendation for a new diet regime she'd recently started—"You should really try it, Simone." At this point, the conversation would pivot toward her: "How's work?" It was always about work. Cynthia loved hearing about Simone's professional life. For her, the world of academia was suspended in golden amber, holding the same shape and color of her own college years in the 1980s, after she'd broken free from her small-town, trailer-park life: brick buildings, bright-eyed coeds, eccentric and idolized professors regaling a rapt lecture hall. *Energy, discovery, independence, romance*—these were the unspoken words that formed an intractable halo around Cynthia's impression of Simone's working life.

For a time, Simone had tried to disabuse her mother of her romantic notions. She described the dwindling majors, the entitled students, the overbearing administrators, the ballooning class sizes, and declining literacy; the emails, meetings, and grading that consumed most of her time. Once, she even made the intimate disclosure that she no longer liked her discipline, that she never read for fun anymore. But all these details glanced off Cynthia's idealism like blunted darts; she seemed unable to take them in. Her daughter was a professor, and Cynthia needed to believe that this was an esteemed, enviable career, that Simone was doing *important work*, and this would be Cynthia's legacy. She did not pester Simone about wanting a son-in-law or grandchildren. "Don't get married until you finish graduate school." That had been Cynthia's recurrent admonition as Simone treaded steadily through high school, then college, bouncing between majors and various imagined careers. When Simone intermittently brought boyfriends home for a visit, Cynthia disapproved of them all, regarding each with an air of mild disinterest. "He's not smart enough for you," she said about each of them. Even now, as Simone approached her mid-thirties, Cynthia remained apathetic about her daughter's love life. She knew that Peter existed and that he was a "tradesman", but she had not yet met him and rarely asked about him.

Their conversation that Saturday mostly followed the standard template—"Do you remember Lois Schrimpf?" (former neighbor, bowel cancer); "How's work?" ("Fine")—before taking an unexpected turn.

"Our house is on the market," said Cynthia, abruptly.

"Your house . . .?" Simone responded slowly, confused. Her mother didn't have a house, and there was no "our". Cynthia lived alone in a sleek urban apartment in Denver.

"The Idaho house," Cynthia said, and Simone felt a space hollow out in her gut as her breath shallowed.

"It's on the rental market, vacation rentals," Cynthia continued. "You can just book it! On this website." She paused, waiting for a response from Simone that didn't come. "There are pictures. It looks good. Almost the same. But the furniture is all different, of course."

The conversation ended shortly after this exchange, Cynthia clearly disappointed in her daughter's aloofness. After hanging up the phone, Simone found herself mechanically opening her laptop, searching for Idaho vacation rentals, and within moments she was looking at her old house, the house she'd lived in between the ages of seven and seventeen, the years of her girlhood, the years at home with her mother. She clicked through each picture, keenly scanning each image, unsure what she was looking for, only aware that she was searching for *something*.

It was a beautiful house, that was certainly true: a 1920s farmhouse surrounded by acres of rolling land, less than a mile from a fork of the Snake River. The stucco house was painted white when she lived there, with a brick-red front door. Behind the house, on the horizon, the sharp peaks of the Grand Tetons jutted into the expanse of the sky. The farmhouse had two symmetrical gables on either end, pointed gables that mirrored the shape of the distant mountains. One of those gables, the westward one, had been her room—a long room like a bowling alley with a steeply angled ceiling. Two rooms, really; there was an inner chamber and an outer chamber, with an open doorway between them.

Most of the pictures showed the house layered in snow, clearly trying to appeal to the ski bums, and it was probably a hard sell. As idyllic as the setting was, the house was remote, a satellite of an isolated town two hours from the posh resorts and ski runs of Jackson Hole, on the sparsely populated Idaho side of the Tetons.

BOOK NOW! The blue button beckoned, and she watched the cursor pull toward it without her consent, like the planchette on a Ouija board. She clicked. Up popped the months of December and January, each day blank as an open door. All available. The house stared at her through the portal of the computer screen, waiting—but not with expectation. Satisfaction.

Conscious thoughts began to surface then, each affirming the decision that had already been made. *It will be nice to get away. I need a break. The snow is so beautiful this time of year.*

That's what she keeps thinking about as she trudges through forty-three analysis papers, flagging comma splices and awkward transitions; as she submits grades, triple-checking each letter carefully; as she packs her suitcase full of sweaters and wool socks; as she kisses Peter's closed eyelids and leaves her townhouse in the predawn dark: the Idaho snow, stretched out like a shimmering sea, covering the gray bones of winter, masking the world's transitory death.

Two

She's misjudged the snow—misremembered, actually. In the half-light of her memory, this Idaho world she'd once inhabited is like a snow globe: cozy and sparkling, easily grasped. But not so in reality.

Vast. That is the word that springs to mind and lingers there as she drives south from Bozeman—a city, analogous to the peopled terrain she's grown accustomed to—and into that remote corner of southeastern Idaho.

Vast.

In her memory the mountains are closer together, not sprawled apart like this, edged against the horizon and separated by hundreds of miles of empty land. No, not truly empty—just bereft of people.

If I drive into a ditch here, I'm stranded, I'll die.

She remembers now—too late—how her mother would keep the car packed with emergency supplies in the winter: heavy coats, a sleeping bag, water, a flashlight. Just in case the snowdrifts grew too tall to burst through, in case the car was pulled into deep snow, marooned there.

It is windy here, windier than she remembered, because of all that open land. Blizzard country.

She's grown used to lights, bright city lights that burn through the night and make an overcast sky glow purple. And hills—not mountains but rounded and walkable, hills full of houses that make the world seem smaller, that make her feel kept and safe. Her eyes are not used to seeing such an *expanse*. She feels dizzy, vertiginous, like she is standing on the edge of a cliff.

This is the sublime, she thinks, remembering her Romanticism seminar in graduate school. There's a name for this: that feeling of an encounter with a terrible, awful beauty that rattles the fragile shell of your mortality. Beauty like a tempest. Beauty that could drown you.

She has about three hours until sundown. That should be enough time. Right now the roads are clear, the sky a vacant white, no snow. *I will be fine*, she tells herself. She hadn't bothered to check the weather, a stupid mistake, she now realizes. She'd rented a car on impulse, the cheapest available, leaving the city in a hurry, like she was trying to catch something—or was something trying to catch her? Either way, she drove as if she was running out of time, as if there was a window closing. And perhaps there is: She thinks of the white paper pharmacy bag nestled deep in her suitcase before pushing the image away. She pulls her attention back to the landscape, the blur of evergreen, the black road cutting through a sea of white.

I'm from here, she says to herself. *This is my homeland.* She almost whispers the word aloud. Who is she trying to convince? Not herself but the land, the land that is entirely indifferent to her presence, to whom she is just a passing metal blip, an insect.

She tries thinking about Peter, about the calluses on the soft beds of his hands, rough against her skin. She pictures his face, but the image is blurred, out of focus. Does she love him? Already he feels like a memory against the domineering presence of this place. The sixteen years that separate her life *now* from her life *then* begin to fold together, collapsing like a paper fan. She is descending, driving deeper into the valley, but is she also moving backward in time?

She needs a cigarette. The craving comes unbidden; she hasn't smoked in years, not since those angsty grad school parties: late nights, gin and tonic, intellectual conversations that slowly derailed into nonsense, headache the next day.

So different from the undergrad bacchanals with cheap beer in red cups, no conversation possible over the thump of loud music pulsing through the walls, fumbling caresses in a stranger's bed. All was immediate back then, the present like a black hole that swallowed everything else. Tomorrow would worry about itself; there was only this neverending night.

Not so in grad school. Pessimism about the future was the uninvited guest to all those gatherings, sitting like a pompous caterpillar in the center of the room, blowing smoke rings and whispering enigmas. The undergrad friendships were turbulent but full of devotion. The grad school friendships were rivalries, pure and simple. There weren't enough opportunities for everyone. Some would sink in the academic job market, some would swim; most would float along from one piece of detritus to another.

She pulls over as soon as she sees a gas station, knowing it will be the last one for miles, perhaps even the last one until she reaches her destination. At first she isn't sure the station is open; it is part of one of those mountain oases—a cluster of buildings huddled together, surrounded by miles of nothing. A diner, a gas station, a long-derelict motel, a few trailers. The diner is closed, the trailers dark, but the gas station offers its neon Open sign as a beacon. Fishing licenses and fuel, likely the only raisons d'être.

She fills the half-full tank, partly out of prudence, partly to hide the fact that she is mostly stopping for cigarettes. Camel Lights. She doesn't want the smokes of her grad school years—American Spirits—but goes all the way back to *then*, to those first furtive puffs, illicit and treasured, the smoke cocooned in her mouth, breath shallow. It wasn't the nicotine blast in the lungs she wanted then; it was the thrill of transgression.

"Don't make 'em anymore."

"Excuse me?"

"Camel Lights." The attendant turns around, eyeing the bright wall of cigarette packets, pulling one down and tossing it on the counter. "Camel Blue. That's the closest."

"Oh." She picks up the small box slowly, looking down at the unfamiliar label. "Okay."

"You on pump two?"

She nods, wondering why he bothered to ask. She's the only one here. It's just the two of them.

"Where ya headed?" He isn't looking at her. He is ringing up the gas.

She hesitates, wondering whether she should lie, thinking about the deserted miles between here and there, the sky beginning to darken. But what could she say instead? Along this rural, two-lane highway, there is nowhere else to go. Her town is the closest town, the next isolated haven.

"Fall River."

"No kidding? Most people go right through there, on to Jackson Hole or Idaho Falls. You ski?"

"No."

Then why are you here? is the unasked and unanswered question.

The attendant leans forward then, resting his forearms on the counter, looking up at her through thick gray brows, lowering his voice, which carries a hint of warning. "I don't suppose there's any way I can talk you out of it?"

She steps back. *What does he mean? How does he know?* She glances toward her car instinctively, making sure it is still there, waiting by the pump. She'd left it unlocked, keys in the ignition. "I'm sorry?" Her voice cracks.

The attendant nods toward the package in her hand. "The smokes. Any way I can talk you out of it? If you haven't had a pack since they got rid of the lights, no reason to start now."

"Oh!" She looks down at her hand, still clutching the cigarettes. There they are, the reason she'd decided to stop in the first place. "Don't worry," she says. "This is just a one-time thing. A special occasion." She swipes her card before sliding it back into her wallet, then tucks the Camels inside her purse.

"Oh yeah? What's the occasion?"

She is already in the open doorway, stepping into the cold. She calls back without turning, letting the wind carry her words as the door floats shut with a jingle. "Reunion!"

It is dark by the time she pulls into town. *Mother will be worried*, she thinks, before remembering that her mother hasn't lived in this town for almost two decades. No one is waiting for her. She will be staying in the house alone.

The gateway to Fall River is a flashing red light, not a full stoplight, just the electronic equivalent of a stop sign: *Pause here, please; briefly acknowledge the existence of this town before you pass on through.*

But she isn't passing through. She turns off the highway and toward the town, the small cluster of buildings huddled along a railroad track. Population 997, boasts the small green sign, a number unchanged since the last time she drove on this road, a town forever on the cusp of 1,000 residents.

Driving down Main Street, in the sparse halos of occasional streetlamps, everything seems exactly the same: the bank, the motel, the library, the elementary school, the post office. A town big enough to have one of everything, small enough to need nothing more, except churches and bars. Five churches, she remembers, and two bars. She passes the bars, in a perpetual face-off on opposing sides of the street, with dueling blinking Open signs. Then the gas station. The nursing home. The clinic where her mother worked. The cemetery.

And then nothing. She's reached the edge of town and beyond, crossed into the surrounding farmland, blanketed now in snow and night. She's driven through the entire town in less than three minutes.

She is surprised by the dark; she'd thought the snow would glow more, pushing back against the blackness, but the sky is overcast, hiding the moon and the stars that here, in this vast emptiness, can burn so brightly, brilliant clusters of pinprick light. But there is no light for the snow to reflect and amplify, not tonight.

She drives those last five miles by rote, almost in a daze, like she is being drawn, like some invisible cord still ties her to that house and now there is a hand tugging on it, pulling her home. *Home.* She repeats the word under her breath. *Home.*

She doesn't have to pause or squint in the dark or double back; she knows exactly where to turn. Her body knows.

There, take a right. When the road ends, a left.

And there it is—that light on the crest of the next rise. *That's my house, still waiting for me, patiently, all these years.*

Has it been sixteen years? That doesn't seem possible now, that long interim, now that she is on this remote, familiar road, approaching the stucco farmhouse with the big red barn, overcome by the feeling that she's never left.

The light she'd seen from the road was the porch light. The driveway, leading to a small detached garage, is freshly plowed. She is expected. She has been beckoned.

She eases the car into the garage and cuts the engine, leaning back against the headrest, exhaling. *I made it; I'm here.* The cessation of motion after hours on the road gives her a sense of vertigo. She needs to feel her feet on solid ground, to inhale outside air.

But her feet, once out of the garage, do not find solid ground but instead sink several inches into the snow, which spills into the top of her shoes. She's neglected to bring snow boots, she realizes. She no longer owns any.

And the air outside is so cold she gasps. The wind has picked up, chilling what is already well below zero. She hunches her shoulders, pulling her jacket tighter, gathering her body like a shell, shuffling up toward the porch, eyes down, watching the snow clump around her ankles, already numb. It occurs to her that she left her suitcase in the car; for a moment she's forgotten that she is a guest here, that her belongings are stuffed into a bag in the trunk, rather than awaiting her in the house.

The house! A thrill goes through her, disbelief, elation. She reaches the porch steps and begins to ascend, feeling as though she is about to lock eyes with a familiar face. She looks up—then stops, mid-step.

The front door—something is wrong. She draws back instinctively. This is not the door she knew. Soon after they moved in, her mother had painted the door a bold brick red. "To match the barn," she'd said. But the door has been repainted, and the shutters too, she guesses, unsure in the murky light. Not red but black, black against the stucco white—a trendy color combination, popular in those modern farmhouse catalogs Cynthia keeps piled neatly in her bathroom.

She must have seen these changes in the cheery, daylight pictures on the website, but up close and in the night, they seem alien, ominous. The black door does not seem like a door at all, but a gaping hole, an open mouth. The light from the porch projects outward, not down, illuminating the path to the porch but leaving the front door in shadow. She hesitates, steps back, for the first time on her long journey confronted by a whispering but frantic voice, somewhere deep down, imploring her, *Turn back now! It's not too late; there's still time.*

Then her eyes land on the gray lockbox hanging from the doorknob. Heavy and metal, so bulky and clumsy and *real* that her visceral unease—the dread, the rising panic—vanishes. She exhales, grasping the lockbox with both hands, letting the cold of the metal shoot through her skin. She presses in the code from the confirmation email. She'd committed it to memory: 4510. Easy enough. Out springs the key. It seems so vulnerable in her hand, detached from a ring or other keys. Keys aren't meant to be alone like this, floating and disconnected, so easily lost.

She slides the key into the lock and turns it. The door pops open, and she is greeted by a draft of warm air. They've left the heat on for her, the absent owners. Suddenly, she thinks of her favorite childhood movie, *Beauty and the Beast*—the Beast's castle, cursed but alive, full of bustling enchanted objects that keep the place humming. Maybe the house itself is welcoming her, emitting light and warmth in preparation to host—at last!—a living, breathing body. How long, she wonders, since another person has stayed inside these walls?

She walks through the door, closing it behind her, temporarily blinded as her eyes adjust to the darkness. Even so, she feels like she can see; the room is lit by memory. Directly above her is the upstairs hallway that curves down into a stairway on her right. The front room is cavernous and open; her mother, a lover of old houses as well as vaulted spaces, had had the contractors demolish the old, low ceiling first thing, exposing the hall of the second floor above.

Moving counterclockwise, Simone mentally maps the space: Beyond the staircase, tucked against the wall, they'd had a large upright piano, and beyond that, a swinging chef's door into the kitchen. Straight ahead, across the sprawling room, was a wall that ended in a small nook, hiding the entrance to a bathroom. Continuing past the nook—the image plays through her mind like a film reel—was the master bedroom, where her mother slept. And there, directly on her left, opposite the stairs, were French doors leading to another, smaller room, where they'd had couches, chairs, a television tucked into a cabinet. The spacious front room was difficult to stage, and her mother had kept it sparse: a few antique pieces against the walls—a washstand, the piano, a hutch—and in the center a long table that sat in the open space like an altar.

She can almost see the table, right there, in front of her; it was a beautiful piece, a family heirloom, hand-hewn wood with matching chairs that creaked and rubbed against the fir floors. The table had been far too big for just the two of them, but they ate there anyway, every evening. She squints hard into the shadowy half-light, as shapes began to reveal themselves—is that the same table? Could it still be there? But no, that is impossible. She fumbles for the light switch next to the door, reaching where she knew it would be, but there is a knob instead, not a switch at all, and as she turns it, light expands through the room from no clear source, like the crescendo of a sunrise. Recessed lighting, she realizes, as the curtain of darkness lifts and the secrets of the room are disclosed.

Everything is different. The front room is arranged as a living room, a couch and several armchairs huddling awkwardly together around a colorful woven rug. There is nothing to anchor the space, no fireplace or television, just the rug on the floor and the egg-white wall whose blankness is disrupted only by a large print of *Whistler's Mother*. The downstairs furniture has a farmhouse aesthetic—not the clean, sleek modern farmhouse, but country farmhouse: eyelet fringes around the throw pillows, floral prints, the armchairs puffy like newly baked rolls. The French doors into the parlor are still there but obscured by lace curtains. She peeks through, not bothering to turn on a light, and can see two recliners facing a wall-mounted, large-screen television.

This feels wrong; everything feels wrong, like the house is welcoming her, ushering her in—*come! come!*—all the while wearing a mask.

She walks quickly, cursorily through the rest of the house, not bothering to turn on any more lights. She has imagined this moment, playing it in her mind on the drive, picturing herself walking through the front door at dusk, with sufficient sunlight and energy to explore the house and even the grounds: the barn, the vegetable garden, the small orchard of apple trees. In her reverie, the house looked exactly as it did when she left for college, and she'd anticipated a feeling of reunion, belonging.

But now that she is here, the rush of arrival dissipating, she feels an urge to hide, to burrow into some kind of shelter that will protect her against the night and the deepening cold. With each step, each tentative glance through a half-open door, the house feels less like an old friend and more like a stranger. And she, *she* is the one being explored, the one being scrutinized; she is creeping, peering around, and the house is looking at *her*.

This sense of being watched lingers as she goes back out the front door and into a wall of freezing air to collect her suitcase and groceries. She stupidly left her gloves in the car, and her skin burns against the metal trunk handle, her fingers stiff and tight like claws, her body shivering convulsively. She doesn't remember the cold being this aggressive, this hostile. She grabs her suitcase and tries to rush back into the house, shoes slipping on the snow, her footprints from earlier already crusted over with ice. She moves through the cloud of her own breath.

Warmth and sleep, that's all she can think of now. That's what she needs, warmth and sleep. She lets those two words spin through her mind like twin stars, scattering her anxious thoughts and binding her attention. They lead her through the front door again and immediately up the stairs, which she climbs hastily, pausing only to twist the dimmer and plunge the house into darkness again.

Three

Standing in the shower upstairs, but the water won't turn on. Twisting the handle right, then left, then up, down, but nothing. So cold, trembling—and there's someone coming up the stairs! Hiding behind crossed arms as if that will make her disappear, she's naked and can't be seen, not like this.

A lock on the shower door—she sees it, turns it, hears it wrench shut like tightening gears, hands are slippery and footsteps are coming up the stairs.

Groping for the shower handle but nothing there, nothing! Looks up and the showerhead is gone too, hands frantically search, but the wall is smooth and bare and closed to her now, and the shower door stretches up to the ceiling; she's in a box, a glass cage. Reaching for the lock again but it has melted away, just like the handle and the showerhead. Peering through the glass, no, it's still there, but on the outside—*it's on the outside*! And someone is twisting the bathroom doorknob.

Water coming in now, but from where—from where? Warm water from below, bubbling up from below; her feet are wet, she's standing in a puddle, there's no drain; where is the water coming from?

From her. The water is coming from her, flowing from her body and pooling around her feet, and it's not water, it's red and viscous and thick and warm and it's gushing from her body, it's blood—

The bathroom door is opening, someone is coming.

Four

Simone awakes with sun on her face, light streaming through the window, warming her skin. She opens her eyes and closes them again. The room is so bright! Stark white walls catching the light, reflecting it back. She blinks slowly, letting her eyes adjust and wondering lazily, dreamily where she is—then slowly remembering that she chose to sleep in the eastward bedroom. She isn't sure why. The choice was unexpected. The east bedroom had been hers only for a little while, sometime during that last year at home. Before that, she'd slept in the westward room, and the east bedroom had been a bland, innocuous guest room, rarely used. But then she'd moved into the east room after ...

The word comes unbidden. *After.* After what? Now that she is groping around for the answer, she can't remember exactly when she switched rooms.

Never mind! She feels a pulse of energy and scurries across the bed to look out the window eagerly. She is giddy, like a child on Christmas: What will she discover today? What surprises await her?

The landscape is layered with crystalline fresh snow that glows; the world seems reborn, utterly new compared to the dark and the cold that she scurried through last night, a dark that seemed to have its own gravity that pulled and tugged at her, wanting her close. Images of her life—Peter, her students, her research, the white bag in the bottom of her suitcase, her actual reason for coming here—all these had flattened into the periphery of her consciousness, like details from a book she'd read long ago. She is *somewhere else* now, neither the present nor the past, but an alchemy of both, a newfound present in the past, or a past that has broken into the present and somehow reopened. She lets the thoughts of her life back home evaporate. *Home.* Where is home anyway? *This* was her home—the thought comes readily. She owns this place, or rather it owns her, in a primal way, deeper than title or deed. *I never should have left*—the words flit through her mind as she drinks in the bright white of the snow. *Or maybe I never did, not really.* The house seems to agree, humming in approval.

The coffee maker isn't where it is supposed to be. Her mother always kept it on the counter, near the mugs, to the right of the stove. As she stares at the spot—now disturbingly blank, just a bare counter—she can almost smell the coffee. She can almost hear the whirring of the grinder eviscerating the beans, usually the first sound she would hear in the morning, along with her mother's barefooted shuffle. She'd lie in bed, wanting time to roll back under the covers with her, wanting to melt back into sleep; she felt like she could never get enough. But once she heard her mother shifting around in the kitchen below, once she heard the muffled banshee cry of the grinder, she knew there was nothing else to do but get up.

But here, now, *this* morning, her body pulses with energy, so unlike her zombified teenaged self. After finding a demoralized Mr. Coffee in one of the lower cabinets, and a stale, half-used bag of flavored grounds in the fridge, *she* is making the coffee; *she* is shuffling around the kitchen with cold feet. And she can almost feel someone else upstairs, someone in the room above her, in the bed she just left, someone half asleep, yet starting to stir.

She leaves before she knows where she is going and why, carried along by a vague sense of adventure. She has to punch through a snowdrift at the end of the driveway. *Nice try*, she thinks, smirking, watching in the rearview mirror as the house grows smaller, then disappears under the rise. She feels skittish, like she is playing a game of cat and mouse—behind the wheel on a deserted road, all alone, but somehow pursued.

Boots! She needs snow boots. Until properly shod she will still be an alien, an interloper among the weathered natives. *But I'm* from *here*, she insists, as if someone has challenged her, as if a voice has suggested that she doesn't belong.

She kicks her chin up, driving now with confidence, with a sense of mission and direction. There was Stuckey's, she remembers, on Main, a catchall store. They'll have boots. Maybe Mrs. Stuckey will be behind the counter, a little bit older, of course, but still clacking her acrylic nails on the register, peering through bifocals at each receipt before handing it over.

She drives back the way she came the night before, eyes fixed on the curved blue awning down the street; that's where Stuckey's was, across from the hardware store. Only a few parked cars dot the long stretch of Main Street. She doesn't see anyone out and about. She passes her mother's clinic and can't help but stare at it, searching the quiet brick for something—a familiar face perhaps, some sign of life—but it is tucked up and silent.

When she arrives at the blue awning, she is greeted by tarnished windows, through which she can see an open, barren room. The old sign—STUCKEYS, no apostrophe—has been taken down, leaving only the ghostly impression of each letter. She gets out of the car and walks toward the storefront anyway, pulling on the door, then peering with cupped hands through the glass. There is nothing left inside except a row of barren shelves and a For Lease sign resting on the floor near the window, as if it fell a while ago and no one bothered to pick it up.

"Well, shit." Simone turns around, hands on hips, looking up the street, then down the other side. Under the shade of the awning, the air is icy again, and she trembles in her thin jacket—warm enough for West Coast winters, but flimsy here. With a quick glance she'll be easily pegged as an out-of-towner, probably (worst case) as a Californian, one of those wealthy ski bums with a second home. Not that there are many second-homers here. They flock closer to the Tetons, to the slopes, to towns with Starbucks and fine dining and boutiques full of overpriced art. This town can't even sustain Stuckey's.

Still, she hates the thought of being read as an outsider. She wants to blend in but also attract notice. She wants to be recognized.

By some miracle, the thrift store has survived. Simone had missed it while driving, but walking back up the street, stepping carefully to avoid sudden pockets of ice, she notices it sitting unobtrusively where it has always been, kitty-corner to the bank. It is in an old brick building that once served as a lodge for the Daughters of Rebekah; their logo is still carved into the stone: a crescent holding a dove with a three-linked chain. The thrift store is easy to miss because there is no signage whatsoever; it doesn't have a name; it doesn't have regular employees; it doesn't belong to any particular organization but rotates through the care of various groups who man the counter on particular days to raise money. No consistent hours, the shop sits dormant for days on end, waiting for the booster club or the local Scouts to pop in and move some product. Which is why Simone is doubly shocked to see, in addition to its continued existence, an Open sign hanging in the window.

The door to the shop jingles pleasantly as she pushes through it; she's greeted instantly by the musty, thrifty scent of once-clean clothes that have been stewing in a plastic Hefty bag for who knows how long. Interesting how thrift-store clothes, when left alone together, all end up smelling the same.

She can hear someone in the back room, moving boxes around and rustling bags, but no one emerges to greet her, so she begins a clockwise tour of the shop, quickly bypassing the corner full of toys and baby things, which for some reason fill her with revulsion and sadness—the motionless baby swing, a row of hanging onesies, a pile of care-worn and rejected plush animals, all tumbled together in a wicker laundry basket.

She thumbs idly through the shirts in the men's section, thinking briefly of Peter and his closetful of flannel, then pushes that thought away, whisking it down the clothes rack along with the shirts. She skips the women's clothes entirely, discerning in an instant that nothing will appeal, and heads toward a taller rack, tucked back behind a lackluster convoy of furniture—laminate bookshelf, metal file cabinet, orange armchair. *Whisk, whisk*, she flicks through the hanging items, coat hangers creaking and clacking: bridal gown, prom dress, prom dress, coveralls—and there, at the end of the line, a lone winter parka, deep blue.

"Oh!" she exclaims with delight, pulling the heavy coat down and draping it over her body like a thick cocoon. It is too big; it envelops her, hanging almost to her feet, the sleeves covering all but the tips of her fingers. She pulls the hood up over her head, feeling like a little girl playing dress-up, stumbling around in her mommy's dress that drags on the floor, clunking along in her high heels—and that *feeling*, that old thrill of stepping into another self, becoming someone new.

"It's a bit long." A low voice, male—an abrupt invasion of her solitude. She gasps and turns, clutching the collar instinctively, pulling the coat tight around her. There's a man in the room—how long has he been there?—watching her.

"Whoa there." He laughs, holding his hands up as if to calm a spooked horse. "Didn't mean to sneak up on you."

Her fear dissipates, and with it a self-protective shield that had obscured his face, sending only the alert: *unknown male*. In truth, she knows him. He is her track coach from high school, who also taught history and civics.

"Mr. Mallory?" She pulls down her hood, now feeling ridiculous in the oversized coat.

He looks at her quizzically; the recognition is not mutual. He extends a hand, suddenly formal. "And you are ...?"

"It's me, Simone." She waits, expecting a reaction. Nothing. "Simone Stark."

Not a flash of recognition, or even a dawn, but a hazy recollection, a dim glimpse of something still far off. "Oh. Stark. *Sim-one*." He draws out her name in a searching way. "Right."

And in this moment, she realizes the asymmetry of their perceptions. For her, he looms large: He was her track coach, her only track coach, for four long years—formative years, during which she traversed not only the orbit of the track but the distance between *girl* and *woman*. But for him, she is one face in a long, multiyear lineup of faces, one brunette among scores, one pair of churning legs amid a whole pack of runners, rushing endlessly around the track.

She had thought of him over the years, often with a wave of nostalgia, a faint longing for that rush of striving and (occasionally) winning, of belonging to a team, of seeing the quiet approval in his eyes when she set a new PR. His face had crossed her mind, sometimes in active memory, sometimes in dreams—and in that time, she realizes now, he has not thought of her at all.

"Wow, it's been, what ... fifteen years?"

"Sixteen." She answers quickly, then blushes, feels silly for knowing the exact number, for having counted.

"Wow."

She bobs her head silently, starting to sweat now in the coat, but she stays inside it, hiding.

"What are you doing here?" Not accusatory, but bewildered, as if he can't imagine why a person who left this town so long ago would suddenly reappear in the thrift shop.

"I'm—" But the answer is gone, blank. Her reasons for coming back—the true ones, the hidden ones, the outright lies—are all tangled together, unsayable. She only knows, in that instant, that there is nowhere else she could be.

Finally—"I'm looking for a coat." This much is true, and sayable.

"Well ..." He hesitates, and she worries for a moment that he might press her. "Pickings are slim on that front, I'm afraid. I've been here the last few mornings and that's the only coat I've seen."

She nods, shifts her feet. "Do you still coach track?"

"Sure do! That's why I'm here. Raising money for the spring meets. We'll hit it hard as soon as the snow melts. You know how it is."

There is a lengthy, awkward pause.

"What events did you do again? Distance?"

She shakes her head. "No, the 200 and 400. And long jump."

"Right! Right. Of course." He is staring at her, squinting slightly, as if he is looking at a Polaroid photo and waiting for a clear image to surface. She has the sense he is rummaging around for a specific memory of her, something to anchor the conversation, a moment of reminiscence—and finding nothing.

But she, *she* has many memories. The long bus rides—small towns and schools so spread apart around here—the twilight runs, the grueling weeks of conditioning, meeting at the school in the dark of morning to run sprints and almost puke. She remembers how they'd all clamor for the bus driver to play the station with the Top 40 hits, and how Mr. Mallory would belt out the latest Britney Spears in a pitch-perfect falsetto, somehow knowing all the lyrics. She remembers spraining her ankle after a bum landing at the district meet, sophomore year. It was a bad sprain; her ankle purpled instantly and couldn't carry any weight. Mr. Mallory scooped her up and carried her over to the bleachers, then taped her injured foot securely with precision and tenderness. She remembers him finding her once, huddled in a ball under the bleachers, weeping—but why was she weeping? And why *there*? This memory is a fragment. She remembers only the gentle concern in Mr. Mallory's eyes, his admonition that "any boy who'd make you cry like this isn't worth even one of those tears." She remembers Mrs. Mallory, too, and her gaggle of children—how old would they be now? Grown, most of them. They'd come to practice sometimes and to the big meets. Mrs. Mallory would cheer and holler as they ran, as if every member of the team were part of her brood.

"Well!" he says, nodding toward the coat. "What's the verdict?"

She glances down at herself, pulling her attention back to the present. "It'll have to do, I guess."

He shakes his head, grinning. "What in the world made you come back to Fall River in the middle of winter without a coat?"

She smiles back at him, faintly, deciding to let the question be rhetorical. "I don't suppose you have any snow boots too?"

Now he laughs outright, shaking his head. "You know, I just might. What's your size?"

Five minutes later, newly shod in a pair of men's Sorel boots, size 7—"These will be a bit roomy, but they'll last till you die"—Simone stumbles out through the front door, wrapped in her blue cocoon. She turns to wave goodbye to Mr. Mallory, but he's already gone, disappearing once again into the back room.

Five

Where to now? She walks along the edge of the street, trudging through the piled snow rather than on the shoveled sidewalk; she wants to test her boots, feeling impervious, armored. She decides to walk without a clear direction, following only the tether of the memory and steering by impulse.

Turn here. And she's off the main drag, into the rows of residential streets—there's about three of them before the town ends. Fall River is basically shaped like a rectangle: ten blocks west to east, seven blocks north to south, with the highway as the western edge, Main bisecting the middle, and the railroad tracks running diagonal, southwest to northeast, corner to corner. The north–south streets are numbered: First Street, Second Street, Third Street. The east–west streets are all named after trees: Pine, Cherry, Maple, Spruce. She's near the tracks now, walking down Sixth past Pine; just one more block and she'll hit them, so she veers east, down Cherry.

All the houses look the same. Her memory maps seamlessly onto reality here: That trailer there belonged to Mackenzie Clark, who lived alone with her dad. Once, on Mackenzie's birthday, he drove them to some hot springs about an hour away in his truck. They rode in the back, a group of five or so girls, reclining without seats under the truck bed canopy with Mackenzie's dad knocking back one tall boy after another as he drove.

And next door, a small white house with a red metal roof, where Ms. Mills, her old piano teacher, lived with her two boys. Ms. Mills: outwardly polished, thin with perfect posture and graceful manicured hands. Simone learned later, not long after she left, that Ms. Mills regularly locked her children in the basement, where they went without food for days at a time. No one knew. Whenever she'd seen them, sometimes answering the door when she showed up for lessons, they'd been so polite, calling her Miss Simone, extending their small hands in perfect courtesy.

Passing the house now, seeing the slits of the basement windows, she can hear Ms. Mills' voice in her head, counting along with the metronome: *Annnnd one, two, three, four...*

And next door to Ms. Mills—a house she recognizes at once; this is where her memory had been leading her all along. How many times had she walked roughly that same route, starting from the elementary school, and, later, from the high school, falling into step alongside her best friend, Cass, as they skipped or trudged or meandered their way to Cass' house, the house that now stands silently before her.

No longer blue, but stone gray, and all but obscured by the spruce trees in the front yard that have, over the years, grown tall and bushy, their branches joining to form an accidental hedge, an arch behind which the house is hiding.

As soon as she is there, on that stretch of road (no sidewalks) she'd crossed a thousand times, the long line of sixteen years between now and her last visit here—when was that exactly?—folds into the length of a day, a week, into almost nothing. Surely Cass would be inside, happy and expecting to see her, to talk animatedly as she always did, buoyant and childlike, a counterbalance to Simone's melancholic intensity. She is losing touch with the present, Simone is vaguely aware—or maybe she is entering an eternal kind of present, a moment undisturbed by the passage of years, where she is always the same age, hovering on the cusp of womanhood, where time flows like an eddy, circling back on itself.

She walks up the front steps and toward the door, turning the knob before catching herself and remembering to knock (she'd always just walked in). As soon as she does, as soon as her confident *rap-rap-rap* on the door interrupts the silence and her trancelike state, she starts to panic: What is she *doing*? She doesn't even know who lives here—it could be *anybody*! What is she going to say? What does she even want? She isn't prepared—

But the door is already opening, has opened, and the face that greets her is both strange and familiar: Cass' dad. Her mind reaches for a name, fumbles in the dark before grasping... *Bruce*. She knew him, or at least a prior version of him; she is shocked by how old he looks, veiny wrinkles around the eyes, skin paper-thin and sagging, age spots like coffee stains on his forehead and hands.

"What do you want." It is not a question.

"Um, hi, you might not remember me, but"—he's squinting hard, suspiciously—"I'm an old friend of Cass, and I was just passing through and—"

"Cass!" As if he hasn't heard that name in a long time, as if he doesn't want to.

Bruce turns away then, his back to her, shuffling into the dark, but leaving the door open. Simone steps through it, waiting for him to rebuff her, and when he does not, she follows him.

The house is dimly lit, but she knows her way around; she can walk it blind. But as her eyes adjust to the dark, she sees that things have changed. Cass' house had been small, a cozy Cape Cod style, built in the 1940s. A cramped kitchen, two bedrooms—one for Cass, the other for her parents, Bruce and Donna. Like Simone, Cass was an only child, but Cass had a father. Simone remembered him as brash and gregarious, already in his sixties when they were in high school. Cass' mother was much younger. That had always confused her; Donna's youthful beauty and Bruce's age—why had Donna chosen him? Bruce was charismatic, sure, but to Simone he always seemed too old to be a father, too young to be a grandfather—he was more like a wacky uncle, bombastic and jokey, yet always aloof.

Bruce is now sitting at the kitchen table, stooped over a wooden duck, a decoy. With steady hands—she is surprised how steady—he brushes green paint down the duck's head and neck, smooth strokes. He works under a bright lamp, the rest of the house kept dim, but even in the half-light, Simone can see that the entire back side of the house has been remodeled, entirely reconfigured, almost doubled in size. The hallway that once led to Cass' bedroom is gone; the walls have been removed, the entire space opened into a roomy living area with tall windows and a fireplace. The other bedroom—she can see into it through a half-open door—has been expanded to create a spacious master suite, swallowing entirely what had been Cass' room.

"Cass is not here. Obviously. She doesn't live here anymore." Bruce looks back up at Simone, peering through bifocals. "She's grown."

Simone laughs nervously. "Of course, I mean, I know that. Of course she's not here. I just thought—"

What had she thought?

"I thought since I was passing through, I'd stop by and see if maybe she still lives in the area." She pauses. "I haven't seen her since high school. But we used to be close."

Bruce looks at her again, hard this time, as if trying to place her. Then he turns back to the duck, leaning his head into the cone of light, apparently deciding he doesn't care.

"In the area," he repeats. "Depends on what you mean by the area. But not too far away, last I heard. Don't you have her phone number?"

Simone shakes her head. "No. But I remember this one." She nods toward the kitchen, where the phone used to be. "The landline."

Bruce laughs at this, a hard, dry laugh. "The landline! Shit." He sits up abruptly, puts down the paintbrush, pushes back from the table. "Alright. I'll bite." He folds his arms. "What's the number?"

Simone feels a dull heat roll up her neck and into her cheeks. She swallows, closes her eyes, imagines herself back in her own bedroom, pulling the handset from beneath her pillow where she'd hidden it, sees herself dialing the number. "644"—she pauses, then opens her eyes, looking directly at Bruce, emboldened—"5722."

He smirks, says nothing, pulls his chair back toward the table, leans down to scrutinize the decoy. "Well, I don't know her phone number. You'd have to ask Donna." He glances up at the clock. "Should be back anytime. You can look around the house if you want." This surprises her, this openness. Maybe he's sensed her curiosity. "Probably looks a bit different than you remember."

"Okay. Thank you."

Don't you remember me? She wants to say this, to challenge his detachment, suspecting that, in fact, he knows *exactly* who she is—how could he not, considering the years she'd hung around this house, his daughter's dearest friend, sleeping under his roof, lounging on his sofa, foraging in his fridge. But he, for some unspoken reason, has decided to pretend otherwise, to feign amnesia, and she will play along.

She unzips her long coat and awkwardly retreats through the kitchen, which is twice the size that she remembers, the tight square opened now into a long galley with a quartz peninsula, a formal dining area just beyond. All the new updates are sleek and clean and tasteful, but underneath she can still see, or rather feel, the house as it used to be, lurking below like a palimpsest.

Below. She looks down at her feet, at the dark, hand-scraped floors, artificially distressed, and pictures the space under them—have they renovated the basement too? In her memory, the basement was a cavernous hideout, dark and ill lit, with wooden paneling and two small beds built into the walls. That is where she and Cass would retreat, often, especially as they got older, needing more distance from the adults. Cass' actual bedroom had been small and was crammed with dozens of porcelain dolls, all lined up on shelves like a silent army, dresses stiff and elaborate, hands at the ready, hair arrayed in sumptuous curls, eyes endlessly staring. It was impossible to sleep in that room— all those unblinking eyes, and also Cass' sleeping parents just on the other side of the wall. But the basement was tucked away, accessible only via the garage, capacious enough for the two girls and all their secrets.

The door to the garage is still where it always was, at the back of the kitchen. Simone turns the knob slowly, feeling the floor creak under her in admonition. She glances back toward Bruce, who is hunched so far over his work and so still that he looks like a headless corpse propped up in a chair.

She slips through the door and is greeted at once by freezing air and the scent of death—fresh death, the smell of meat from a creature who was recently alive. There, in the middle of the garage, is the carcass of an animal, hanging from a large metal hook. It has been skinned and gutted; only a red-purple body remains, muscle and fat exposed to the air, flesh still united to the bone with white sinew.

She rushes past it, feeling bile rise in her throat, instinctively scurrying down the cement stairs to the basement door, which pops open as soon as she touches it, as if on cue.

It is dark, but she shuts the door behind her anyway, wanting to barricade herself from the raw, metallic smell that has followed her. She blinks slowly as the room emerges from the shadows, reaching around above her head for a small chain that she knows will be there—and it is. *Click.*

There they are—the dolls. Perfectly preserved but shunted to the basement. Row upon row of childlike faces with blank, blank eyes. Ashen skin, glowing pale gray. Tiny red mouths. Arms bent slightly at the elbow, hands reaching out, summoning. They want something. They want to *tell her*, but their lips are painted on and sealed shut; their faces are masks of stone.

Six

She uncrumples the piece of paper once she's back at the farmhouse—to think of it as *home* is so instinctive—and stares at the numbers. Only the area code is familiar; Cass still lives in Idaho, but in a midsized city about an hour away, to which they used to escape and meander the mall.

Donna had given her the number. Donna—so shocked to arrive home, grocery-laden, and find Simone in the kitchen—greeting her with fraught surprise and looking nervously toward Bruce, then Simone, then back at Bruce, before swiftly layering her face and voice with a veil of false cheer. "Simone! I can't *believe* it. How *lovely* to see you again." Donna, rifling through the kitchen drawers, casting a tight smile toward Simone now and then, and barely perceptible glances at Bruce, still bent silently over his work. Donna moved quickly and quietly, like a thief attempting to pilfer something behind a guard's back. Finally, she found what she was looking for, a postcard of Old Faithful with a phone number scrawled on the back. She moved as if to hand the postcard to Simone before thinking better of it and copying the number hastily onto a scrap of paper, which she slid across the counter. "There you go! So good to see you!" Old Faithful disappeared back into the drawer, which glided silently shut. "Thanks for stopping by!"

Simone carried the paper with her throughout the day, deep in the pocket of her blue coat, occasionally reaching down to touch it, to rustle it between her fingers, as if it were a talisman, a rune with powers that could be unlocked, if only she knew the right incantation. She wandered the town like a ghost, unnoticed and unrecognized, her face as blank as the few that she saw, faces that glanced at her, through her, then away.

When she finally does dial the number, she is startled when someone answers, startled to hear another human voice after hours of silence, and the sound of her own voice seems strange. Cass also seems startled, echoing back Simone's words as slow questions, which she poses in disbelief: "You're in *Fall River*? You went to my *parents' house*?

"I'd love to see you," Cass says finally, her first declarative statement. "Would it be possible for you to come here? It's been ... awhile since I've gone down there. To Fall River." *Down*, she says, even though Fall River is north of where Cass lives. They arrange to meet in person for brunch the next day.

Simone had to call the number from the landline because her cell phone has died, nestled dark and silent in the bottom of her suitcase. She keeps forgetting to charge it, keeps forgetting about it altogether—strange because normally she is so attached; the phone is her tether to the rest of life, to other people, to the outside world, and she tends to check it compulsively, like a neophiliac lab rat.

But here, in this buffered, snow-hushed world, the cell phone seems a portal to a place that she is trying to escape, to forget. She wants to sever the tether. Is Peter worrying about her? She doesn't know. He seems able to sense when she needs her space and withdraws to let her have it, waiting patiently for an invitation to return—not restless or eager, just open. Sometimes he looks at her intently with something like wonder, brushing her hair back from her face, tenderly. "You've got a lot going on in there, don't you?" And something inside her snaps shut.

Peter is far away now. Or rather, she is far away from him—days away, miles, and also years. This distance feels different. *Vast.* The memory of him, his voice and his face and his touch, is fading.

She doesn't long for him, exactly, but she longs for *someone*. A warm presence in the house with her, a sense of movement and life. Night is falling and with it comes a dark canopy of seclusion. The only light outside is doubly reflected, doubly diminished—from the sun to the moon, from the moon to the snow. And the moon is half in shadow.

There's someone else here.

She's awake but motionless, body paralyzed, only her eyes can move and they flit rapidly over the room, her ears straining, reaching for the smallest sound. There's someone here, but she can't see him, her head is turned in the wrong direction; she can see the door in her periphery, it's halfway open, but she closed it, she knows she closed it, and now it's open and something is *inside*. Watching from the corner where she can't see, it knows she can't see. Watching and crouching and far away but somehow touching her, pressing her down against the bed and she can't move or turn or scream. A strangled moan escapes her mouth. *Help me*, she wants to scream, but there is no one to help, and the words are caught in her throat anyway, tangled up on her tongue, which is leaden and heavy like a dead person's tongue, like the tongue of a dead deer she saw once on the side of the road, a recent kill, the smooth body intact, and she was mesmerized, mesmerized by the open eye, the glassy eye, she had to touch it, something made her touch it, and it wasn't hard like she expected but soft, gelatinous, and wide open—not in terror but *absence*, open like a lacuna, a chasm, open like a freshly dug grave.

"So, what's good here?"

"I'm not sure—I always get the same thing!" Nervous laughter.

They are hiding behind their menus, shy, like a first date.

Simone orders coffee, her third cup already, even though it's not yet noon. She slept badly again, feels like she can't wake up. Her stomach is rumbling, eager for a second meal already. She hopes Cass can't hear.

"So where are you staying?"

"At my house. I mean, my old house. It's a vacation rental now."

Cass' large eyes widen at this, and Simone remembers that look, that childlike amazement, how easy Cass has always been to astonish. "Wow. What's that like?"

Simone shrugs. "It's weird how normal it feels. Like I never really left. Except the furniture is all different. And the mattress sucks. I feel wrecked." More jittery laughter.

"I can't believe you're *here*. This is so trippy. But, like, *why*? Don't get me wrong, I'm happy to see you, but why'd you come back?"

Whenever someone asks her this, the inevitable question, her mind snaps back like a rubber band to the real reason, the secret reason, the reason she has made an effort not to think about. But is that even *the* reason? Or is there a reason beneath that reason, something deeper and more profound, some invisible force pulling her here like gravity? She returns to the script.

"Well, I needed a writing retreat, and what better place to hole up than here in the snow? And my mom found our old house on this vacation rental site. I don't know ... It was kind of an impulse, to be honest."

"Wow, what are you writing?"

Another question Simone dreads, because nonacademics assume it must be something interesting, like a novel that might become a movie, rather than an obscure analysis of seventeenth-century poetics that five people will read. Mindlessly she describes the article she is working on, wherein *working on* means "occasionally thinking about and not yet writing or even researching". It is always helpful, in her circles, to have an interesting-sounding project ready in the holster, to be "working on" something, even when the truth is that she is burnt-out: on teaching, on writing, on theory, on the fraught and disintegrating realm of the humanities, which is always desperately trying to prove its relevance and desirability to the world, like a clingy girlfriend who can't accept the message, *Look, we're just not that into you.*

While they wait for their food, they talk around the unspoken things, moving in wide circles through safe topics, reviewing the demography of their current lives. Cass: graduated from Boise State, now lives with her fiancé in Idaho Falls, works as a speech pathologist, no kids, two dogs, runs marathons. Simone: bounced around the United Kingdom collecting various credentials, now lives in Oregon with Peter, teaches literature at an urban university, no kids or dogs but a quadruplet of degrees.

There is an absence of competitive energy as they exchange these litanies; Cass seems sheepish talking about her races, and Simone tries to muffle the word *Oxford* with a mouthful of biscuit. They both appear to be hiding, peeking shyly at each other around their résumés, curious and full of questions, but afraid to ask about anything real.

Eventually, when they are well into the meal, picking slowly at what remains on their plates, Simone ventures toward a topic that they've both been actively avoiding: the past.

"So, have you kept in touch with anyone from Fall River? Who's still around?"

Cass sits back, exhales. "Let's see. Who's still around...?" She smiles wryly. "You know, not many. We all kind of scattered. You went the farthest and the fastest—I remember you taking off for Europe or wherever after graduation and thinking, *Well, that's it for Simone; she's not coming back.* Then your mom left not long after, right?"

Simone nods.

"I wondered if that made it easier for you to move on like that, since you weren't born here, don't have family here. For most of us, it's hard to get out."

Simone feels a twinge at this. They'd moved to Fall River when Simone was seven; her memories of life *before* are blurry and disjointed, a series of apartments in various Western states as her mother finished her residency and took a string of temporary posts. Fall River was the first place, the only place, she ever put down roots, but because she was a transplant, not a native, she remained an outsider.

"Still," Cass goes on, "most of us did get out, to one degree or another. Except for the farming families. Farms and the school, that's what keep people there, for the most part."

"Yeah, I saw Mr. Mallory."

Cass' face lifts for a moment. She'd been the star of the track team; lean and lithe, she could outlast anyone in the distance races. "Oh yeah?" Simone watches as Cass seems to disappear for a moment into a memory, wistful. "He was the best."

"Do you keep up with him? He must be proud. I mean, you ran in college and now you're doing these marathons."

Cass shrugs. "I did during college, for a while, but not so much anymore. It's hard to keep tabs on people unless you're on social media, and I'm not, really."

Simone nods. "Yeah, me neither."

The waitress comes to clear their plates, filling Simone's mug to the brim with fresh coffee. Simone watches the steam curl into the air.

"Did you see Adam?" Cass asks.

Adam. And just like that the sound of his name is moving through her ears and down her throat, hot like a shot of whiskey settling into her heart, which starts to beat faster.

"Adam?" She echoes his name as a question.

"Yeah, Adam." Cass laughs at Simone's apparent confusion—which is not confusion at all, but the slow dawn of something long dormant beginning to stir.

"He works at the nursing home. Or at least he did. He's an RN. Coaches girls' basketball too, I think. At the high school."

"Adam." She says the name again, then laughs at herself, mainly to hide how agitated she suddenly feels. "Wow. I haven't thought about him in a long time."

Cass shakes her head, bemused. "Yeah, *Adam*, you dumbass, the love of your frickin' life. How could you have forgotten?" Cass is laughing at her now, eyes alight, no longer hiding; they've fallen into an old rhythm. "How many *hours* did I spend listening to you talk about Adam this and Adam that; oh Adam is so sexy, oh Adam hates me, oh Adam I want to have his babies."

"Stop it." Simone is laughing too, at herself, at Cass, in relief at the sudden dissipation of tension. Their guards are down now, the air feels easy. "It wasn't that bad!"

"Oh my gosh, yes it was. I wish I could beam you back there so you could hear yourself."

The waitress has brought the bill, but it sits between them, untouched. The meal is over yet seems to have just now begun.

"He's a nurse? Seriously?"

"Yup. Last I heard."

"So, honestly—when's the last time you were up there?"

Cass hesitates, either searching for the answer or reluctant to say it. "Five years."

"Five years! Really? Why? I mean, it's only an hour away. And your parents still live there."

Cass nods. "That's the why."

"Oh."

"Yeah. We're not really talking right now. When you called, I was surprised. Not just because *you* called, but that you got my number from *them*. I didn't even know they had this number."

"Yeah, well, your mom kinda had to dig for it." Simone lets the silence sit for a bit, hoping that Cass will volunteer answers without her having to ask. No luck.

"The house is really different. Have you seen it?"

"No, but I saw the plans before—well, last time I was there."

"Your room is gone. It's been swallowed by this big master suite."

Cass smiles, wryly. "Yep. Sounds about right."

"It's nice. I mean, well done. Whoever did the remodel did a good job. It's just weird. The house looks the same from the outside, all small and cozy, and then you walk in and it's a different place entirely. Spacious and huge. I mean, it *echoes* now."

There is a pause. "Did you see my dad?"

Simone nods, feels Cass' words pull taut with tension. "Yeah, he was the one who let me in. But he didn't seem to remember me, or at least he pretended not to, for some reason." She notices that Cass' face has changed, lapsing into a blank mask. "They still have all your dolls, though." Simone wants to console her. "They're down in the basement."

Cass looks at her, alert now, eyes rounding in horror. "The basement? Why would you go down there—how could you go down there?"

Seven

Adam.

This is the first word that surfaces as she emerges from sleep, the word that alights on her forehead, her lips, soft like a butterfly. She whispers it aloud.

The night has ebbed, and with it the undertow, even its memory, the undulating fact of its existence. Forgotten.

How had she not thought of him until Cass spoke his name yesterday? How had his memory not been shimmering in her mind like a mirage since the minute she descended into the sweeping valley that holds Fall River?

The memory is there now, and far more dense, more tactile than a mirage—her body remembering his body: his long-fingered hands, calloused on the palms but soft between the fingers, hands large enough to encompass her own, the rough hands of a quarterback, a farmer's son, yet tender still.

She remembers that homecoming, junior year, his first game as starting quarterback. He'd asked her to wear his jersey that day, game day, and she'd worn it proudly, the bright blue and white, his last name stretched across her shoulders in gold. She walked down the hall between classes slowly, regally, stretching out the minutes of being looked upon enviously by the other girls, thinking all the while in a frenzy of bliss, *I matter, I matter.*

They lost the game, a brutal, humiliating defeat by their rival, crushed 36–0. Yet nothing could dislodge the stars from her eyes, which remained locked on that jersey she'd worn all day, locked on the budding man who wore it on the field. She watched him stand tall, arm cocked to release a pass that remained in potency as he was slammed into the ground by the defensive blitz, over and over and over. A martyr, he seemed to her: dragged down by the lions, yet rising to be mauled again, a tragic hero.

He met her in the parking lot after the game, wordless and dejected, his eyes darting away from hers in shame, trepidation. She beamed at him, saying nothing yet everything, the adulation in her face meeting his humiliation, easing it, her coy smile, irrepressible, teasing out a spark, a question.

The silence continued as he drove her home, not heavy and fraught but electric, buzzing with expectation. His right hand, so impotent during the game, now rested on the bench seat of the truck, angled toward her in a gesture that seemed casual, meaningless, but she knew it was an invitation. She held herself away, huddled against the door, not daring to touch him—wary not of him but of herself, of the fiery spiral in her abdomen, coiled tight and ready to spring.

They were on the back roads now, a mile from her house, glancing at each other in the darkness, lit only by the unseen moon. He slowed down, way down, coasting to ten miles an hour, leaning toward her, hand still on the wheel, and he covered her face with kisses, her face suddenly close to his, lifted upward and toward him like a flower finding the sun. His kisses were soft and quick, little bursts of delight—so different from the boy who'd kissed her behind the bleachers the previous winter, whose tongue had invaded her mouth before making a swift retreat. She'd never even learned his name. Adam's kisses were different, like he was giving something to her, rather than taking.

She can feel it now, that inward inferno, as she lies sprawled on the bed, eyes open and staring, fixed on the ceiling but seeing only the past.

Two hours later she finds herself driving to his farm, his family's farm, without realizing it. She is driving there without having decided to drive there. *This is fate*, she thinks, *this is the gods*. She is merciless in the hands of a power greater than herself, hands that have tied a string between her and the man she is seeking. She is not choosing; she is being chosen. The knot was tied long ago, and someone is pulling on the string.

The day is overcast, the gray-white sky an unbroken extension of the ground, aside from the occasional interruption of unburied fence line. The snow is growing ever higher, often imperceptibly, like a glacial flood, a frozen water line inching upward—and then, in a blizzard, taking a great leap. But deepening, always.

Despite the enveloping white and the buried landmarks, her memory fumbles forward, each mile illuminating the next, like a dark pathway lit by a flashlight beam, one step at a time. She's a good ten miles from town now, headed east. Soon the domesticated squares of farmland will dissolve into feral forest and gravel roads. She can see the Tetons to the southeast and feel the unseen edge of Yellowstone to the north. But this is the backside of all that, the doorless borderland, far from the fanny-packed tourists who flock to experience the still-wild West.

Where was that turn . . . ? And as soon as she asks, she sees it, knows it, turns north, and the road dips down, crosses the river. His family farm is on the next rise; in less than a minute she'll be there—and then what? She's been moving on instinct, almost in a trance, and now she startles awake; there are no other vehicles out here, no visible house or farms, no reason to be on that road except to visit the Hoffmann farm. What is she going to do? Ring the doorbell, talk to his parents? Probe for Adam's whereabouts? To what end? Why is she doing any of this? What is she looking for?

The questions spiral together, moving from her anxious mind down into her gut, where they sink like little rocks. She slows down instinctively, wanting suddenly to hide, to burrow into the snow and disappear. Only half a mile to the farm now. She searches anxiously in the rearview mirror, wondering whether she can turn around in the narrow road, then imagines her rear wheels sliding into the snow and getting pulled into the concealed furrows on either side—she's in a Fiat for Pete's sake, a puny, untested rental car—and then she'd *have* to ring that doorbell and ask for help, conjure some reasonable explanation for her presence, for which there is none.

She has slowed to a complete stop now, idling in the road, unable to move forward or to go back. And then she sees it: movement up ahead, at the farm, a pickup moving slowly down the long drive. It reaches the road, turns its broad nose toward her. Panicked, Simone lurches into motion again, sinking down into her seat, keeping her eyes fixed straight ahead, just above the steering wheel. The truck passes, but she doesn't dare look at the driver, afraid of the magnetism of her eyes, a met glance. Instead, she looks away, at the passing expanse and the tree line beyond. The truck passes—she tracks it in the rearview mirror—and crosses the river, turning west toward town.

Simone herself has reached the driveway to the farm, newly plowed, and uses it to make a quick U-turn. When she reaches the main road, she can still see the pickup in the distance, easily visible, a dark speck heading into an abyss of white. She turns toward it, pressing gently on the gas.

She follows the truck all the way into town, hanging back as far as she can while keeping her eyes on her mark. The past few miles have seen the occasional car on the road, and she's relaxed more, feeling less conspicuous. There is nothing strange or noteworthy about being on a rural highway headed into town in the middle of the day, after all—*wait, how is it already near noon?* Time flows differently here: the hours painfully slow at night, then skimming over the surface of the days like a flat, spinning rock.

The truck turns onto Church Street, a road true to its name, home to five different churches along a short stretch: first, the Lutherans; a little farther on, the Baptists and Methodists facing off; next, the LDS stake center, and finally, the tiny Catholic church, Our Lady of the something or other.

She thought the truck might be headed to the elementary school, but it surprises her by easing to a stop across from the Catholic church. There is nothing else on that block *except* the church, but why would anyone be going there? It is Monday after all. *Who goes to church at noon on a Monday?*

She pulls into the LDS lot down the street and parks behind a large pine tree, watching the pickup to see who will emerge. Until that moment, when the truck parked at the church, her heart had fluttered wildly with the hope that it *was* Adam in the driver's seat, that maybe he'd been visiting his parents, or maybe he actually lived there, maybe he'd taken over the farm, something he swore he'd never do, but maybe . . .

But Adam driving twenty minutes into town to go to church on a weekday? She can't help but laugh aloud at the idea. The Hoffmanns are Catholic, she is now recollecting, but Adam had never seemed into it, not even that one time when she went to Mass with him for a special ceremony, some kind of spiritual milestone. She remembers the priest dipping his thumb in oil and tracing little crosses on their foreheads—Adam and the three other kids up there. She sat through the Mass next to Adam's mother, awkwardly mimicking her gestures but always a step behind, later ambling along with the Hoffmanns as they went up to get the little discs of bread, keeping her arms crossed over her chest like a sleepwalking vampire, as she'd been instructed. She remembers avoiding Adam's eyes, knowing her face would erupt into a smirk—or, God forbid, some kind of crazed, irrepressible laughter. She stared at the giant crucifix behind the altar instead, letting her eyes explore the disturbingly realistic form pinned to it: the sinews of its long, gaunt limbs; the body tight with pain, expectant; the head drooped in resignation. How macabre, she remembers thinking, yet she was unable to look away. Her gaze was drawn to the almost-corpse compulsively, the way her eyes would leap and fix on bloody roadkill by the side of the road even as her mind urged, *Don't look, don't look.*

They'd laughed about the whole thing together later, entangled in the cab of his truck. "You're the only sacrament I need," he'd said, his lips on her ear. She had no idea what a sacrament was, but in that moment, she knew she wanted to be one.

The driver's door of the pickup opens, and a person climbs out, too small to be Adam. It's his mother, Helen, smaller and more stooped than she remembers, but still the same cropped hair and oversized flannel shirt. She hurries across the street with not even a glance back toward Simone's car. Helen clearly hasn't noticed the Fiat silently tailing her for the last ten miles, eyes set only on her destination, which she now enters, disappearing through the wooden doors.

Simone climbs out, swathed by her voluminous blue coat, and trudges across the street, head down. The wind has picked up, pushing against her as if trying to drive her back, keep her away. But away from what? She is trailing Helen without any clear goal in mind, simply following the aimless current that keeps pulling her along, vaguely hopeful that some deeper purpose will unveil itself when the time is right. She is questing for a quest.

Besides, aren't Catholic churches always open, waiting for the stray wayfarer who needs a quiet, half-lit place to unburden before God? Or is that just in the movies? She asks this as she pulls on the front door and it releases toward her. Open. She ventures in, her coat gently rustling, and finds herself in a narrow, musty vestibule with a small table covered in pamphlets and a rack of plastic rosaries. She reaches out to touch one, drawn by the bright beads, blue like her coat, and quickly, without thought, ushers the beads into her pocket.

That's when she hears the bell, an actual bell, pealing out like an alarm, as if she's been caught stealing or trespassing or both. She glances around frantically, heat moving like a wave up her neck, into her cheeks, body tensed and already anticipating reproof from some gaunt priest or hardened nun who has materialized silently behind her, but—nothing. She's alone. Had she imagined the bells? Now, ears piqued, she can hear the murmur of human voices, buzzing in tandem like a hive. She cautiously approaches the interior double doors, moving her head toward the narrow beam of light streaming between them, guiding her left eye to peek through.

There's a priest in a purple robe bending over the altar, kissing it; a gray-haired man in white off to the side, carrying a large crucifix on a pole, now wrangling it into a stand; in the pews, a smattering of bodies, maybe a dozen altogether, standing and watching the priest, now sitting in unison, responding to some unspoken signal.

There's a Mass going on. Do they do this *every day*? She'd thought the Baptists were excessive, with their services on Wednesdays and Sundays. "Maybe it's a Christmas thing," she whispers aloud, her breath billowing around her face, a warm cloud in the chilled air. The vestibule is not heated; she can feel the warmth from the sanctuary leaking through the doors only to dissipate immediately, consumed by the cold.

Two sets of double doors and a small space between, heat and frost seeping through on either side. She could backtrack easily, go out the way she entered, back out into the vacant air, back to the rental car, to the rented house, to the game of pretend she's playing with herself, all to avoid the ominous thrum of the real, the distant knock that she can *feel* rather than hear, deep within her, that ticking clock. It has proven harder to hide here than she'd anticipated, in this yesterday town, even with the snow-muffled quiet and the layers of icy white continually entombing everything anew. Even so, nothing seems to stay buried.

Or she could go forward, continue this reckless, goal-less quest, cat-and-mousing with the past. Maybe the two choices are the same. Maybe the doors lead, ultimately, to the same place. But in this moment, warmth seems better than cold; a strange sanctuary preferable to an empty house; the presence of strangers more tolerable than absence.

She opens the door just enough to wedge herself through, misjudging the expanse of her coat, which scrapes loudly against the doorway. She ducks her head and scurries to the least obtrusive corner, the farthest end of the back pew on the left-hand side, the least populated side. When she dares to lift her head, after a solid minute of bending low in what she hoped looked like prayer, the faces she had imagined—no, *felt*—were fixed on her in disapproval weren't looking at her at all, but still turned toward the front. Her entrance, her *incursion*, had not disrupted the strange spell that kept them all attuned forward—toward what, exactly, she wasn't sure. Was it the priest? The crucifix? Or maybe that gold domed box behind the altar, the thing that looked like a prop from *Raiders of the Lost Ark*?

She regrets her decision to enter as soon as she sits down, but it's too late. Leaving would be too disruptive. She stares at the back of Helen's head, poised to duck and hide her face if need be. Perhaps Helen will lead her to Adam somehow, but not willingly. She has to stay hidden.

All morning, she's been moving by impulse, never quite letting herself stop and think about where she's going or what to do next. But now she's stranded, marooned in the one place in Fall River that holds almost no memories for her; she might as well be sitting in a strange museum. Perhaps that in itself is a kind of refuge, a chance to regroup, buffered from the past.

She leans back, letting her eyes and mind wander. There are so many weird things to look at, so many images. The last time she set foot in a church was several years ago, at a college friend's wedding. She reaches for the memory—it was an Episcopalian church, or Presbyterian, something with a *p* sound. Aside from the pastel ebullience of wedding décor—cascading flowers, fairy lights, candles—the sanctuary had been quite stark: clean lines, dark wood against white walls, lots of arches gesturing upward, a large domed window overhead, translucent with clear-paned glass. Was there even a cross? She assumes so but can't picture it. *This* church, the space she now inhabits, is almost cluttered by comparison.

There are bodies everywhere, and not just the one on the crucifix. On either side of the main altar are two statues, one masculine, one feminine, both holding a child, but in different ways—the woman cradling the child, his ear against her heart, the man holding him up and outward. "Jesus, Mary, and Joseph," she whispers wryly, staring at Mary's painted plaster face, which is lowered demurely. *Virgin and mother at once*, she thinks. An impossible ideal. She remembers her graduate seminar in medieval literature, the cult of Mary, her professor's conviction that Mary was a male fantasy, brilliantly concocted to control women while seeming to elevate them.

Her mother would have liked that seminar. She can hear Cynthia's voice rattle through her mind as she glances around the room, feeling a faint adolescent thrill at having voluntarily chosen to enter a place her mother would detest. Not that Simone enjoys being there, not that she's even *comfortable*, not in the least, but the source of the thrill is transgression rather than delight.

Cynthia had always been particularly contemptuous of Catholicism. "Superstitious and puritanical," she'd say. "Always trying to control women. Steer clear." This was one of the reasons she disapproved of Simone dating Adam, or at least the most convenient excuse. The disapproval would have been there nonetheless, once the crush bloomed into longing, simply because Simone belonged to Adam; she had given him her heart. Unlike the parents of her friends, who would have been dismayed to learn that their child had a homosexual orientation, Cynthia seemed displeased with the idea of her daughter having *any* kind of sexual orientation—but to fall for a *Catholic boy* was the worst-case scenario.

In Cynthia's evaluative taxonomy of religious groups, Buddhists and Quakers were at the top, in the Acceptable category. "You don't even have to believe in God to be a Buddhist or a Quaker," she'd say, offering this as a mark of distinction. Reformed Jews and WASPs were Neutral, potentially respectable and ultimately harmless, indistinguishable from secular humanists. Mormons, Hasidic Jews, and Evangelicals were Unfavorable—the former because of their reckless fecundity, the latter because of their politics. But only Catholics sunk to the level of Loathsome, arousing all dimensions of Cynthia's animus for their superstitious rituals and procreative profligacy. "Any woman who's a Catholic is brainwashed," she'd say. "If you have to go through a religious phase, that's fine. Whatever. Just don't be a Mormon or a Catholic. To be Mormon, you'll sacrifice your brain. To be Catholic, you'll be enslaved to your body. And trust me, there's nothing worse."

Simone can hear her mother saying these words, the harsh staccato of her conviction, as she glances around the cave-like sanctuary and notices that, aside from the two men up front, there are mostly women in the room with her. It's almost all female voices murmuring the prayers that they somehow all know, without even glancing at a book, without even opening their eyes. There's Helen, with her roughened farmhand aesthetic; a few white-haired grandmotherly types in thick sweaters; a petite *abuela* flanked by what could be her daughter and small granddaughter: two generations moving in unison, wordlessly taking turns holding the lively, wriggling third. Near the front, there's another woman, hunched either from age or devotion, Simone can't tell; the woman's face is hidden under a spidery black veil that hangs from her head in a stiff triangle. The only man in the room, aside from the priest and his assistant, is a younger Hispanic man, perhaps her age, in full gray coveralls with a hand-stitched name tag she can't quite make out. She wonders idly why he would choose to waste his lunch break going to church. Guilt, probably. Maybe he went on a bender over the weekend.

The priest is at the podium talking now. Several women had trailed up there first, reading from something; then they all stood up while the priest's assistant read some more. Now they are all sitting again, and the priest is talking, this time in his own words. He's a short, stout, balding man with round spectacles balanced on the edge of a beaked nose that seems all the more angular against the general roundness of his form and features. He speaks quickly, with a thick Mexican accent, and when Simone finally turns her attention toward his words, all she hears is the word *porpoise*. "You have a porpoise," he's saying, "a God-given porpoise. For you, God has a porpoise. For *you*." He points with emphasis here, in her general direction, and abruptly she sees the image of a smiling, buoyant, dolphin-like creature leaping its way through wide-open water, its body a single, pulsing muscle barreling its way toward her, frisky with excitement and trembling with devotion, coming for her, meant for her, made to love *her*, just *her*: her very own porpoise, sent by God.

Just as her imagination sees and welcomes this image, delighting in it, she realizes the priest is saying *purpose*, that God has a *purpose* for her. But *purpose* is so abstract, disincarnate yet somehow weighty, like an anchor or a yoke, something she has to drag along behind her—nothing like the exultant, gravity-defying creature arcing through the air and water and flashing her its wide grin.

Thanks, but no thanks, she thinks to herself. *I'll take the porpoise.*

Eight

She sneaks out once they all start moving toward the front in an orderly line, keeping her head low, shuffling back through the double doors and into the snow, which is falling listlessly, drifting down to the ground. What had been the point of all that? Following Helen for miles back into town only to watch her go to Mass. What was she hoping for? That Helen would lead her straight to Adam? Does she even *want* to see Adam?

Yes. A spark of a yes, a flicker, deep down, the only clear and unambiguous thing she's encountered since—when? She is not used to *yes*. She is not used to hearing that clear bell strike in those rare moments when she stops to listen to her inner rhythms. She is used to hearing *what if?* and *I'm not sure*, or just silence. When had she last followed a yes—her own, not losing herself in someone else's? This life she is living, this methodical, linear life of the professional woman climbing the Ladder of Success, achieving goals to unlock new goals to achieve—she's been feeling burnt out, yes, but surely she's not *just* her job. She has a *life*, she has a boyfriend—no, not boyfriend, she is an adult, she has a *partner*—she is multifaceted and interesting, she has *hobbies*, she is doing that thing called work-life balance; she is *balanced*. All these goals she's been chasing over the years, like a trail of breadcrumbs sprinkled by someone else along a path made by someone else—who? She's met all the milestones, one by one, not faltering once, despite her ennui, not until this moment, when, looking back along the path, the path she followed away from here, away from

Adam, she hears a question arise in her heart: What if this was all a detour from the life she was *meant* to live? A life of love, of devotion?

No! She has outgrown the fairy tales; she is educated, dammit; she is a *critical thinker*; she knows how to read past the magic and the enchantment and the happy consummation of lovers, the naïve ever after. She knows how to peel all that back and find the dark realism below: the grubs of prejudice and patriarchal power, the writhing anxieties about death and loss, the detritus of existential dread, plagues and such. There is no such thing as destiny; she and Adam had been accidental lovers, and here she is, pining for an accident, trying to force an intersection of their long-separate paths, trying to curate fate.

Yet she can't help imagining it: seeing him, falling back in love, uprooting her life, shedding the academy, trading the pursuit of achievement for a small-town life, close to the earth. Like a movie reel it plays through her head: the love, the children, the growing old, the side-by-side burial in a plot of familiar land. What if she's been wrong all along? What if her mother was wrong, her professors, the high-achieving women who had ushered her along, shaping her in their mold, guiding her choices to validate their own. What if they had all heard this *yes*, this call at the center of their being, just like she was now, only to greet it with a *no*?

Perhaps this was *the moment*, the call to adventure, that initiating moment of the hero's journey. She'd taught it so many times in Lit 101, that archetypal narrative pattern that appears in every culture, every great story: the hero's journey. And it begins with a call to break out of the confines of ordinary life and into something *more*. Many try to resist the call. The risk is too great. What will be her answer?

"Simone?"

She turns at the sound of this voice, her eyes meeting the broad, German face of Helen Hoffmann, mother of her first love, who is coming toward her now in what seems to be the urgency of disbelief, that instinctual need to verify or contradict the witness of the senses, to touch the apparition.

"Simone, is that you?"

"Yes."

Nine

They are standing face-to-face outside the church, underneath a statue of the Virgin Mary flanked by several chubby winged babies, all with upward eyes fixating on a mound of crusted gray snow piled on Mary's head like a Zhivago hat.

"Why are you here?" The incredulity in Helen's face has hardened into suspicion.

For a few seconds Simone had wondered if the call she'd heard had been heard by Helen too—perhaps this moment was kismet, a mutually anticipated and longed-for reunion, a coming restoration of the might-have-been.

But there is no gratitude or welcome in Helen's eyes, only wariness and something harder underneath, something bitter.

"I'm here for work."

"Oh? There's not much work around here. Especially in December."

"No." Simone laughs, momentarily amused at the implication that she would come here for seasonal agricultural work. "I'm here to finish an article."

"About this place? What's there to say?"

"Not about this place. I just thought this would be a good place to write."

"In December."

"It's very beautiful in the snow. And quiet."

This was the longest she'd ever had to justify her cover story. Most people were satisfied by now. Not Helen.

"There's a lot of beautiful snowy places, most of them quiet."

"Well, I know this place."

"Do you? How long's it been? Fifteen years? It's not the same as it was when you were here."

"It looks the same."

"I'm sure it does. From the outside."

That arrow lands, that familiar arrow. Simone has always been an outsider and always will be. No matter that she grew up here, became a woman here, fell in love here; no matter that her mother spent over a decade tending to the ailments and illnesses of the good people here, mediating their births and deaths. Simone and her mother were always on the outside.

"Are you Catholic now?"

"What?"

Helen tilted her head toward the door of the church. "Saw you at Mass."

"Oh no, no." She laughs again, despite herself, struck again by the absurdity of what Helen thinks is possible. Perhaps they really do live in two separate worlds.

"Maybe you thought you might run into someone here? Someone you used to know?"

Helen has stepped closer to her now; she is half a head shorter than Simone but somehow still looms over her. Simone's excuses, both rehearsed and impromptu, bubble up in her mind but remain unspoken. Her heart has quickened, harnessing all her energy; her throat snaps shut like a trap.

"Look, Simone." Helen's voice is low and gentle, but somehow her words still slice. "There are some things that shouldn't be dug up. Especially when you're the one who chose to bury it." She gestures at the statue as she says this, at those innocent cherubs gazing heavenward, as if Simone has somehow offended them.

Simone reddens and looks down at her feet, feeling the hot bile of shame and rage rising in her gut. *How dare she ...?* She doesn't look up as Helen walks away; they part in silence,

Simone staring down at her ridiculous oversized boots, as if they will keep her steady and anchored to the earth, so much more substantial than the dainty nubs of Mary's feet peeking out from under her stone robe. She looks up at the statue, at Mary's arms lifted out and up, presumably in prayer or offering, but which now seems to Simone like an exaggerated "who knows?" gesture, especially with the hat of snow hanging low and hiding her eyes.

Simone waits in the car, head bent down, until Helen's truck has receded from view, turning toward Main Street and out of sight. Then she sighs, all the tension and potency of her anger and desire whooshing out of her in single, prolonged expiration. How quickly it had vanished, whatever that was, the wellspring that had overtaken her as she stood outside the church.

She can still feel the taste of that yes—how *good* it had felt welling up within her, a wave of hot, animating energy building and cresting, about to cascade its way through her entire being—until Helen hit, like a splash of cold water in the face. Helen, with her dubious, level stare that zeroed in on the girl behind the mask. And just like that, *epiphania interruptus*. Her yes folded back in on itself, burrowing down into an ossified shell, hardening into a no.

No. She is not here for some higher purpose. She is not meant for some romantic destiny. She is not about to be swept up into some adventure, some epic love story. Her choices, her actions, are not weighty and significant—*fateful*—not part of a higher story, some cosmic tapestry, some *destiny*; no, they are unbearably light, weightless, like the flakes of snow tossed in the air outside and onto the windshield, each fractal unique and exquisite, but only for a fleeting moment before disappearing utterly on the glass, never to exist again.

Surely there is a psychological explanation for all this, for her momentary insanity, for her inexplicable decision to come back here in the first place, to do what she had come to do *here*. Or maybe there is an evolutionary explanation, some resuscitated instinct deep in the reptile brain, to burrow and hide, like a dog who tunnels into a darkened corner under the porch when she's about to give birth.

Well, whatever the impetus, whatever firing neurons or imbalanced chemicals drove her here, here is where she is. And there is only one thing left to do: get it done and over with, the thing she came to do, then drive back into her life, her real life that is patiently awaiting her, unsuspecting and, as yet, undisturbed.

She puts her gloved hands on the steering wheel, gripping it hard in grim resolve, and cranks the wheel to the right, her mind already racing ahead of her, tracing those long miles back to the house, where she will carry out the choice she has already made, which, once done, will weigh on her for only a little while before melting entirely away.

The wind has picked up, gusting hard from the north, barreling against her little car that was not made for weather such as this.

What is wrong with you? Why didn't you rent something with four-wheel drive? The harsh, berating thoughts come flooding in now, flying at her like the on-rushing snow, the blurring streaks of white, heavy now and getting thicker. Blizzard weather. *There's no hospital in town. What if something goes wrong after . . .?* This was a terrible plan, an ill-fated impulse. *You have lost your mind.*

For the first time since her departure, she feels an urge to call Peter, to hear his steady baritone voice, which always has a calming, anchoring effect. "Come home," he'd say. "We'll figure this out together."

She can picture exactly what he'd be doing right now, what he would be eating for lunch, how he would be spending the evening, what friends he would be meeting, what game they would be half-watching, what beer he would be (moderately) drinking, what time he would head home and go to sleep.

That's part of why she'd fled here, to evade that steadiness, that predictability—not because she disliked it, no, the opposite: She was afraid of unsettling it, afraid of knocking things off-balance and unleashing life-altering chaos upon them both. She'd come here to protect him, to protect them both, to preserve the form of their life, which had developed into something almost whole: a smooth vessel of unfired clay, all but ready for the kiln.

That's why I am here, she reassures herself. To keep her life with Peter intact. And she can still do that, she can see it through and then go back to him, to their unbroken circle, their seamless world of two.

How close she'd come to almost destroying it entirely! Until only a few minutes ago, she'd been possessed by the prospect of being swept away from that life, of being caught up into a turbulent river of fate and carried into another life entirely, a life that might have been hers once, a shadow life that for an intoxicating moment had seemed inexorably real.

The visibility is terrible now, so different from the clear calm of midday, when she'd trailed Helen into town. Now she is moving blindly through a tunnel of white, hands like claws on the steering wheel, eyes fixed on the twin ruts ahead of her, the only place on the road where the pavement is not yet buried. If she can keep her tires in those tracks, she'll be okay—she'll stay on the road. If not, if she slips even a little, the snow will pull her off the road and into an irrigation ditch, those deep traps flanking either side of the road, hidden beneath the layers of frozen white.

How deceptive the snow can be, making everything look even, making you think the terrain is solid and level, dependable, and then ...

Just as she thinks this, just as she lets herself drift into rumination about the witchery of snow, her attention skips and her hands waver and the tires slide just an inch too far to the right, and, quicker than a breath, her world tips sideways; she's lying flat against the passenger door looking up at the blizzard through the driver's side window, which now sits above her like a submarine hatch.

Her first impulse is to sit there, uncomprehending, dazed by how quickly the whole world has swung sideways. How often this has happened to her in dreams: Her most common dream motifs involve sudden glitches while driving, usually the brakes not working, no matter how hard and repeatedly she presses her foot onto the pedal with all her strength—the car, immune to her control, barrels through the red light or the stop sign or over the side of the bridge. But in her dreams, these are usually slow-motion disasters; the car keeps moving against her will, but everything else slows down, and she becomes strangely buoyant, light; the careening toward death turns into a balloon-like descent that ends mercifully as she reunites softly with the ground, unharmed. Other times the slowness simply means more time for terror, for that gradual dawn of awareness that she is about to die, she is flying through the air in a moving metal cage and she will crash into the earth or the sea or the cold, dark river and she will die. In these less merciful dreams, she awakens at the moment of death—not gasping awake and sitting up violently, but rising up and surfacing like something that has been submerged. She wakes to find herself in the grip of a whole-body response to imminent death, which feels something like being in an elevator that is falling too quickly, her heart and stomach and bowels wrenching sickeningly. To reach the surface of sleep—to break upward—while still feeling one's heart and guts and life plummeting downward, this is the worst kind of vertigo.

But the real-world accident, unlike the tortuous dreams, happens in a flash, too quick for conscious awareness, let alone dawning existential dread. By the time she understands what has happened, it is long over. Dread and rising panic are not the prelude but the aftermath, and she is feeling it now, panic—first as only a wordless, physiological sensation, but quickly accompanied by thoughts: *You are alone. You don't have a phone. No one knows you're here. No one saw. You are trapped in a sideways car in a blizzard, and no one is coming to help.*

But then, perhaps because she'd just been thinking of Peter, of his steadiness and calm, another, saner part of her rises to the occasion, attempting to soothe the roiling body and the frenzied thoughts. *You will be fine. It's the middle of the day. Someone will drive by and see you. You're not gonna die. You're just stuck in a ditch.*

Simone closes her eyes and decides to trust this voice. She burrows into her thick blue coat, never so grateful for its downy warmth, its capaciousness. She retracts her hands into her sleeves, tucks her knees up and her chin down, curling up into an embryonic ball and taking shelter.

The wind howls outside, whisking the snow from the ground, swirling it into the air again, casting it elsewhere. It won't take long for her car to be half-buried in weather like this. She's about three miles out of town amid a flat ocean of farmland. Inside the car, the air is still and quiet, the only sound the hush of her breath and the occasional rustling of her coat. She wonders how long the car will stay warm, but this is a distant, idle musing, not urgent. She becomes aware that a calm has settled over her, as the panic of the accident has dissipated. There is a part of her, surprisingly, that seems glad to be here, glad to be stranded in this unchosen pause, this purgatorial waiting, unable to keep driving back toward the house and the packets of pills waiting expectantly in her suitcase, which is zipped up tight and pushed under the bed.

A thought comes to her uninvited, maneuvering past her defenses—that she's not actually alone. The choice that has felt so inevitable has not yet been made. It's not too late to unweave this row in the tapestry, a row not yet finished, the threads not yet tight. The mirage of yet another possible future emerges: one different from the one she planned while coming here, the one that would be kept open by the pills in her suitcase, but also different from the one that had called to her earlier, outside the church, before Helen intruded with her deadening severity. There is a third option, another possible pattern, one of neither passion nor caution, but something else—what? She searches for a word but comes up short. Of the three, this dream of a life is the most inchoate, mysterious. Unsettling. Yet it presents itself, nonetheless, as a possibility. To accept the unexpected, come what may.

Ever since she found out, she's felt trapped, like the speaker in that doom-laden line from the Sylvia Plath poem: *boarded the train there's no getting off.* Yet here she is, actually stuck in a car that's rolled into a ditch—and it's only in this moment that she considers, for a fleeting moment, that she's not trapped at all, but free. Three possible paths unfold before her, and she is free to act, to pursue one over the others.

She knows what her mother would tell her to do. She knows what Helen would say, with her Catholic hangups. But Simone, herself, what does *she* want? The call to adventure is supposed to be clear. There is a quest, a task, a destiny. Unwelcome, perhaps, but unambiguous. Instead she is bombarded with options, the weight of multiple futures, which is exactly why it is restful, in this moment, to be marooned in the present. She does not want to act, she realizes. She wants to be acted upon. She wants to be swept up into a force greater than herself, carried along by a river that has carved its way into the earth over millennia.

Maybe chance can be her destiny. *Rock, paper, scissors.* Can't play it alone. (*See, you* are *alone*, she tells herself.) She fumbles around in the car for a coin but finds nothing. She can't remember the last time she's carried cash.

But she does find the pack of cigarettes, pristine and wrapped in cellophane, tucked safely in the center console. This will do. Camel side up, she takes the pills as planned. Camel side down, she stays on the train, rides it to the final stop. "Do you want to get smoked or not?" she asks the camel. "Your fate hangs in the balance too." And she flings the pack upward, flicking her wrist to make it spin, watching it end over end, heart hammering as if the results of this absurd divination will be binding. But she's used too much force. The pack bounces off the driver's side window above her, ricocheting into the back seat, where it falls unseen.

"Dammit," she whispers, reaching her arm under the passenger seat to fumble around and find where the cigarette pack landed, so she could see *how* it landed, so she could discern the murky terrain of her own conscience and desire. Which result is she hoping to see?

There's a sharp *rap* at the window above, a face peering through, a man's voice. "Are you okay?"

Simone rolls up onto her knees like a penitent, calling through the window, "Yes! I'm here; I'm okay!"

The man pulls on the door handle, then calls back to her, "It's locked."

Never has she been so eager to unlock a car door and let in a total stranger. She stretches up tall, still on her knees, and reaches up to push the button and release the lock. She can't yet clearly see the man's face, which is shadowed in the halo of a fur-lined hood. Even his voice comes to her distantly, words coming apart in the wind. But he tries the handle again and pulls the door skyward, opening it against gravity. Somehow he braces himself, using one arm to keep the door open in the punishing wind, while reaching down his other arm to her like a rope.

She grabs on with both hands, one up by his bicep, the other grasped in his broad, gloved hand; her feet find holds on the steering wheel, the headrest, as she climbs her way out.

"We'll have to leave your car." He has to shout over the wind, gesturing toward his truck, which is parked up on the road, hazards blinking. But the flickering red barely cuts through the white haze. The lights are only visible up close. Simone realizes how easy it would be to cause a pileup, how dangerous it was for him to stop and help. She tries to move quickly, climbing down from the car into the ditch, but sinks immediately, hip-deep in the snow, her heavy boots like anchors. "Here," calls her rescuer, and she's grasping his arm once again, drawing on his strength. He ushers her into the passenger side of his truck, and it is only in the seconds that it takes for him—a dark, hooded figure—to walk around to the driver's side that Simone begins to question her blind faith in this stranger, into whose hands she's entrusted herself.

He starts driving immediately, checking the rearview and side mirrors, not yet pulling back his hood or looking in her direction.

A sensation rises up from behind her sternum, a tremulous wave, quelling all movement—heart slowed, breath shallowed—cresting into a thought: *I've been here before.* Not *here* in this exact truck, but *here* in proximity to this body—younger once, but the same rope-like arms, lean and strong. *Could it be?* The knowing of her body is held at bay by the doubting of her mind. *There's no way.*

She can't stop herself from glancing at him, trying to see the still-shrouded face, wanting, *willing* him to look over at her, but he stares straight ahead.

"I can pull off up here," he says, as the dark hulk of two granaries emerges into view, looming over a small farmhouse. "Do you need me to call an ambulance? Are you sure you're okay?"

He glances at her then, and she catches a glimpse of his face—it's wrong somehow, like a mask. It's not the face she expected to see.

"Yes," she replies, her voice hoarse. "I mean no. I mean yes, I'm okay, and no, I don't need an ambulance."

The man turns off the road toward the granaries, the already half-buried driveway marked by a pair of yellow poles. The truck's heavy tires grind easily through the drifts, which are about six inches high and growing, motionless ripples of piled snow.

When she thought it was *him*, her body had coiled in anticipation; when she saw that it wasn't, that tension dissolved, rushing out of her like an exhale, leaving her body heavy with disappointment. Now, as the driver shifts into park, letting the engine idle, she can feel herself constricting with a different kind of expectation, a low-grade trepidation. The intimacy of the small truck cab, which had for one long moment felt so natural, so familiar, now seems confining. This stranger so close to her, his hands on the wheel, the white-blind world outside—she is trapped, at his mercy. She remembers the sensation of his arms as they gripped her, pulling her out of her car; the strength had been comforting then, but now ...

The man pulls back the hood of his parka, half turning to face her, looking at her with intensity, eyes narrowed. Then he points at her. "Wait."

Simone presses back against the door, her right hand reaching for the handle, ready to take her chances with the hostility of nature, when the man's face clears with the openness of recognition. "You were just at Mass, weren't you?"

"Mass?" She echoes the word as a question, as if midday were the distant past. Time seems to move differently here, expanding and contracting like an accordion, the past breaking into the present, and the present fading quickly into hazy, far-flung memory.

Then it clicks. This must be the man from the church who was wearing those coveralls. She never got a good look at his face.

"Yes! That was me." She laughs nervously, trying to ease the tension, but her laugh sounds frantic, high-pitched.

"I'm Miguel." He stretches out a gloved hand. She takes it.

"Simone."

"Where were you headed? I can get you home if it's not too far, but if you were headed toward Driggs or Idaho Falls, you're probably gonna need to wait this out, find someplace in town."

"I'm staying just down the road. It's not far. Maybe a couple of miles."

Miguel nods approvingly. "Great." He shifts into gear and the truck ambles forward, moving slowly back onto the road, the high beams able to illuminate only about ten feet ahead. "I knew we were getting a blizzard today, but this . . ." He leans forward, peering hard into the whiteout, shaking his head. "I haven't seen a storm like this in a long time. Once it clears, I can tow your car out. But it probably won't be until tomorrow."

"You don't have to do that. I can call someone."

He laughs. "If you call the nearest tow place, my boss will answer and send me out. There's only one auto shop in town. That's where I work."

"Oh! Well, I guess I lucked out."

"We'll probably be busy tomorrow, but I'll get your car as soon as they plow."

"That's really kind of you. I mean, you don't have to go out of your way or anything." She tries to relax, to feel grateful, but her mind is still roving suspiciously, scanning for possible threats. Why is he being so nice to her? Does he expect something in return? She clears her throat, tries to make her voice sound steady, confident. "I can pay you, of course."

"Nah," he says. "Afraid I can't let you do that."

"Why not?" Her voice is high-pitched again, the voice of an anxious child.

"Well, Father told me to do an act of charity today. You know, as a penance. And if you pay me, that doesn't exactly count, does it?"

Charity. She's not sure how she feels about this, being someone's good deed, an instrument to ease a guilty conscience.

"Penance, huh. Did you do something wrong?"

Miguel glances at her with a wry smile. "Of course," he says. "Don't we all?"

Ten

The storm outside is still raging, has been for hours. The blizzard cold has seeped into the house, into her bones. Ever since climbing out of that ditch, hanging on the arm of a total stranger, she hasn't been able to get warm. Maybe a bath will help, the warm water a kind of enveloping presence, a surrogate companion.

She heads toward the master bathroom, wanting to sequester herself from the tempest outside, which seems, with each raging gust, to be testing the house for weakness. But when she gets to the doorway of the bedroom, she stops abruptly, as if she's stepped against a wall of ice.

There is an invisible boundary at the entrance of her mother's room. She always sensed it when they lived there, every time she stepped through. Even now, as she stands at the threshold of the master bedroom, a room adorned in alien décor—gaudy floral patterns that her mother would detest—even now, the room feels like her mother's, just as the house feels like their house, owned by others but marked irrevocably by *them*, by their long years there.

There was no such barrier to Simone's room; the boundary was completely porous. The whole house, really, had been like a spacious antechamber of her mother's bedroom. Cynthia held all the keys and went where she wanted, without a knock or even a pause. She possessed the house.

There were times when Simone was allowed into the inner sanctum where her mother slept—when her mother wanted to spend time with her, or when they folded laundry or tidied together. The room was always spotless and sparse;

she remembers speaking in hushed tones instinctively, as if the room itself could not tolerate noise or dust or disruption of any kind, its taut white cleanliness too fragile and liable to snap.

She remembers one such time when she was fourteen, already three years post-menses and enduring the total rebellion of her body: breasts distending, hips spreading, her face spotted with tiny pink pustules. She was a mountain in the midst of eruption. *Obtrusive*—that was the best word for it, how she felt, struggling to hide inside a body that refused to be hidden.

They were making the bed, the two of them, a mother-daughter dyad smoothing down the sheets in tandem, tucking in the corners, hands moving in mirrored gestures, wordless synchronicity. Simone could feel her mother looking at her, assessing.

"Did you see the book?"

Simone nodded, avoiding Cynthia's eyes. A week or two earlier, she had arrived home from school to find a book on her bed entitled *Explaining Sex to Your Teen*. That night she called Cass to read excerpts aloud in her best British radio voice, pausing frequently to muffle her hysterical giggles with a pillow.

Had Cynthia overheard her phone call with Cass? Simone swallowed hard.

"Do you have any questions?" Cynthia was still looking at her.

Questions? *All* she had were questions, and they clamored in like noisy children. *Will it hurt? Is it bigger than a tampon? How will I know what to do? What if I don't want to do it?* But she shushed them away, *quiet, quiet*, shaking her head. No questions.

Cynthia nodded, satisfied. She turned toward the door and Simone followed her, relieved that they appeared to be exiting the conversation.

Then Cynthia stopped in the doorway, turned back. She locked eyes with Simone. A charge seemed to move through her, through her and into Simone, a shock of electricity.

"If you ever get pregnant, I'll kill you," she said.

When her period came, that's when things began to shift. She remembers the moment, turning to find a cloud of red-brown liquid in the toilet—not bright but muted, so much that it took a moment to recognize it as blood. Her heart began to hammer—was *it* happening? to *her*?—and she called out to Cynthia, brought her in to see.

"Hmm." Cynthia's mouth was thin and tight, a hyphen. Two apostrophes appeared above her eyebrows, staccato grooves. Simone had learned to read her mother's face like a meteorologist, catching minute signs of shifting weather, impending storms. The appearance of those tiny lines, etched with tension, was not auspicious.

She had expected, what? Not joy. Her mother rarely showed joy, but satisfaction perhaps, or at least a nod, an acknowledgment that that day, that very hour, Simone had stepped from one world into another, not by skill or willpower, but by the hidden gnosis of her body, which was beginning to speak a language she had not yet deciphered.

"I think I have some pads somewhere," said Cynthia, who no longer menstruated, having had a hysterectomy after Simone's birth—or during it, really, quitting herself of both child and womb at once. "That ship has sailed," she'd say, whenever Simone pleaded for a younger brother or sister. "I only wanted you."

After combing through the bathroom cabinet, Cynthia found a stack of three maxi pads that had been sent as a sample in the mail. The pads were thick and bulky, feeling less like something Simone was wearing than something she was riding. She waddled awkwardly, like a sore cowboy, astride a ponderous foreign object that rustled with each step.

A few days later, once the bleeding had stopped, Cynthia took Simone into the clinic, early, before it opened. "Just want to look things over," she said. "Nothing to worry about." She did this on occasion, ushering Simone through a battery of unnamed tests referred to only as "routine". Simone learned from a young age not to bother with questions or objections. It was easier to acquiesce, to lie down on the papered bed compliantly, bored out of her mind, as Cynthia measured, inspected, and prodded.

That particular morning, Cynthia drew Simone's blood, filling two separate vials, and x-rayed her wrists. Then, for the first time, she asked Simone to lie back and put her heels in the stirrups. "Just want to make sure everything's okay down there," she said. It was over quickly, perhaps five minutes, through which Simone winced, feeling her muscles tighten, her body recoil; she closed her eyes, imagined herself as a crustacean, pictured retracting her limbs and head into a hard, protective shell. Then it was over, Cynthia was done, and, wordlessly, they drove to school.

Cynthia never told her what tests she'd run or what results she found; she never said whether or not everything was indeed okay, and Simone had the impression—never directly confirmed—that things were not okay, that there was, in fact, something deeply wrong with her, that her body was wrong, that this moment she naïvely thought was a rite of passage, a portal into *womanhood*, was instead a perversion, a malformation, a falling away.

It only got worse from there. That first period was a herald of more dramatic changes to come: the soft fur that colonized her body, from her upper lip down to her ankles; the pockets of fat that ballooned on her chest and hips, bending her familiar rectangular form into the shape of a violin. Her body felt like it was *spreading*, oozing past its boundaries, newly soft and voluminous. She was used to running and feeling the lithe buoyancy of her limbs and muscles, so light and free that she didn't think of her body as a body, but just as *herself*, the seamless extension of her will. But now, it was heavy, cumbersome, metastasizing at an uncontrollable pace. It was an *it*. She began avoiding herself in the mirror, scuttling away from her own reflection like a nervous animal. She couldn't bear to be seen, even by her own eyes.

The mirror of Cynthia's face was even worse. There, Simone saw her own inner turmoil—shame, betrayal, disgust—manifested in her mother's features, a damning confirmation. Cynthia was as disturbed as she was. The simplicity of their life, the mother-daughter dyad, was being upended—not just by Simone's external metamorphosis, but by her internal turbulence.

The heat and fire of Simone's nature, docile and dormant for so long, easily quelled with a harsh look or a dousing of bitter soap on the tongue, was quickening now, churning; she was volatile, molten with rage and desire, anguish and ecstasy. The predictable pattern of their life together, the synodic rotation of *daughter* around *mother*, her blank face that dutifully reflected, never burning with its own light—this primordial system, older than her murkiest memories, was, for the first time, destabilizing. There was another gravitational force emerging, one that could contend with the force that held her in orbit: the fusion of nuclei in the core of her being, the white-hot fire in her heart.

There Simone stands now, lingering in that same doorway, flooded with memories—a grown woman, yet frozen in place. *I am a grown woman*, she tells herself, but the words are a punchline to an absurd joke; someone is cackling at her, *You are a joke.* She tries to summon her age to mind—thirty-two? thirty-three?—but the numbers ring false; time has folded back on itself, that much she knows, dragging her along in its undertow.

The undertow. That is her secret name for this nameless feeling—the quiet darkness that hides below the surface of her life, waiting to surge up and swallow her. She closes her eyes, steadying herself by pressing her hands into the doorframe, letting the feeling fully surface: the dread, the pain in her sternum, the skull-pulsing pressure, like the weight of deep water, building and building as if the doorway is getting smaller and the walls are tilting toward her, as if the house itself is closing in.

This is a feeling that has haunted her over the years, bubbling up like groundwater and pulling at her on occasion, usually when she is overworked and overwhelmed. But sometimes it springs unbidden, rushing in to spoil a perfectly placid day and suck her down into the muck.

And now, suspended in the doorframe, just outside her mother's room, letting the undertow sweep in and take her, she remembers: *I used to feel this way all the time.*

Eleven

She takes a long bath in her mother's tub. It is still there—an antique ivory bathtub, held gently aloft from the floor by four clawed feet, huge and brass, each capped around a ball, like the claw of a griffin clutching an egg it has snatched from an untended nest.

Only on rare occasions had she been allowed entrance into this tub; her mother's bathroom was like a sacred space, the bathtub especially. Her mother had found it, a real coup, at a cluttered antique store in West Yellowstone, stashed in a corner, full of folded quilts. It was after the tub arrived that Cynthia became more protective of her bathroom, disappearing into it each evening with a teeming glass of red wine and a paperback. Cynthia picked up used romance novels from thrift stores, read them once, then threw them away. They never earned a place on the bookshelf, and Cynthia kept them away from Simone. "Not appropriate for young girls," she'd said, even when Simone was in high school and going through a banned book phase. Cynthia never seemed to care what Simone read, but romance novels were off-limits, which was fine with Simone, who as a teenager was already developing elite literary tastes. But this had always perplexed her, her mother's romance novel habit, especially considering that Cynthia never showed any outward interest in men. She'd never had a relationship, or even gone on a date, while Simone was growing up, and as far as Simone knew, that hadn't changed. And it seemed as if she would have preferred that way of life for

Simone as well. Just the two of them, mother and daughter, a closed sphere of intimacy that no man need broach. Until, of course, Adam.

Adam. This is the thought, the memory, that possesses her attention as she reclines in the tub, submerged up to her neck in hot water, so hot she'd had to inch her way down into it, one limb at a time. For one moment today, she'd been sure she was in Adam's presence again, close enough to touch him, and that moment had continued to expand and open, a well of gravity swallowing up all the other moments of the day, which now seemed meaningless. She had felt, in that moment, a rare sense of certainty: *This is where I belong, this is where I am meant to be, all my life has led up to this.* Then the voice and face of a stranger broke in. The moment—which had begun to feel like a portal, a gateway to another life—snapped shut, all the conviction rushing out of her, leaving only a lack, a gaping absence.

But the moment isn't gone. It is still with her now, still there, not lost but closed, a door that could, perhaps, be reopened. After all, he is here, in the orbit of this town somewhere, maybe only a few miles away. What is he doing right now? Is he thinking of her? No. Back in Oregon, she'd rarely thought about Adam. He belonged to the past, and Peter was her present. But coming here, everything seemed upside down, inverted. *I could come back. I could reenter this world.* These are the kinds of thoughts surfacing in her now. And she is starting to believe them.

The wind wails outside, pummeling the windows; the storm is still surging, as it has been all day and now into the night. Aside from this, the house is quiet—but a tense, anticipatory quiet. A waiting quiet. She sinks down even deeper into the water, up to her nose. Somehow, subtly, night has fallen, the whiteout of the blizzard shading into black, a different kind of blindness but blindness all the same. The small, curtainless window above the bath is like a blank, dark eye, rounded in the corners from the accumulation of blown snow.

She lets her eyes close, her mind wander, thoughts drifting idly but always circling back to Adam. What if things had ended differently, what if she hadn't—

A sudden, agonizing creak seizes her attention, not a creak from the windows, from the wind, but from *right behind her*, followed by a finger of cold air on her skin. The door to the bathroom, she knows without looking, has opened. The door that she closed and locked and then chided herself for locking before getting into the tub. *Did I ...?* Yes. She remembers the antique lock above the doorknob, twisting it sideways, the chilled metal.

She wants to turn, to look, but her body is unresponsive, her eyes fixed ahead—but she can see, dimly, in the reflection of the small dark window, the contours of the door splayed open behind her and, as she's staring, an abrupt, shadowy movement, like someone stepping out of frame.

She waits, petrified, so motionless the water around her is like glass. She counts in her mind, slowly, silently, mentally grasping each number like a climbing hold, all the while staring hard at the window for the slightest movement.

Her thoughts begin to thaw even as her body remains frozen.

Miguel. He knows she's here, alone, without a car, stranded in a blizzard. He's the only one who knows. And he could drive in the snow with that big truck if he needed to, wanted to. Maybe he never left after he dropped her off. Maybe he pulled off into one of the empty outbuildings, biding his time, watching her draw the bath and undress, and now he's in the house, hiding in a dark corner, waiting. This was a perfect opportunity, really, the ideal setup for a crime. In the morning any tracks would be brushed clean by the wind and covered with fresh snow.

He could dump her body in a deep drift somewhere, and it wouldn't be found till spring.

She closes her eyes, fear coursing through her, thoughts flickering and landing on strange things, like fairy tales from her childhood where objects and people change forms in times of urgency, and the most urgent need she feels in that moment is to hide her body, for the translucent water around her to solidify into soft blue cloth that she can use to cover her nakedness.

This water has already turned tepid somehow, cooling rapidly. She can feel her exposed skin rippling with gooseflesh. Her teeth start rattling together involuntarily. It is as if, once the door slid open, all the heat was sucked out of the room. She isn't sure how much time has passed—it seems like none at all—but with the water turning cold, it must have been longer. Long enough for the worst to have happened, but it hasn't.

She lifts her arms out of the water, grips the curved sides of the tub with both hands, and pulls herself upright. She turns to look at the door, which is still agape, open wide to the dark innards of her mother's bedroom. What is that shape, there, in the depths of the room, that tall, vertical shadow—human height but too thin to be human? Or is it just one of the posts on the bed frame?

In one quick, liquid motion she leaps out of the tub and rushes to close and lock the door. She hurriedly brushes a towel over her body, fumbling back into clothes still damp, hair dripping. *No one is there. It was just the bed, the four-poster bed.* She waits and listens but hears nothing, only the wind, still thrashing against the house.

Getting dressed has emboldened her; her clothes feel like armor. With a deep breath and measured, methodical movements, she turns on the bright lights over the bathroom mirror, then unlocks and reopens the door. The added light illumines the bedroom enough for her to see the furniture clearly, even if much of the room still lies in shadow. She begins to cross toward the bedroom door, toward the light switch, tuning into her peripheral vision without turning her head. *Walk slowly*, she tells herself, *like a sane person*. The door is closed, just as she'd left it, and with a *click* new light claims the room, dispelling all shadow, exposing every angle and nook, revealing the stark fact that she is definitely alone.

She checks the closet and under the bed, just to make sure. Nothing. In the closet, only empty hangers. Under the bed, only dust.

Now that fear is receding, pulling back from her body like a tide, she feels only a craving for sleep. She turns back to the bathroom, hanging the dropped towel neatly on a hook and flicking off the garish vanity lights. There is still water in the tub, so she bends down to reach for the chain—then recoils, steps back. The water, so glassy and clear when she'd first eased into it, is now clouded and rust-colored, as if tinged with blood. *Must be the old pipes*, she tells herself, plunging her hand into the now-frigid water.

It's only when she stands up, looking through the door into the bedroom once more, that it hits. The bed—placed precisely where her mother's had been, evenly spaced between the two windows. Her mother's bed had four posts, one on each corner, jutting upward like dark, sleek pencils, rounded at the tip but still sharp looking. But this bed, the one in the room right now, is a sleigh-style frame. It doesn't have posters at all.

She remembers the shape she'd seen by the corner of the bed, that outline in the dark: thin and tall, stock-still. *I must have imagined it*, she thinks, *a trick of shadow and memory.*

Is that possible? To remember something into being?

Twelve

She crashes into a deep sleep, into a dream that she's in the house, but the house is underwater; she's exploring, swimming from room to room, looking for something, somehow able to breathe, as if the water is her natural habitat; she dives down like an arrow to wriggle through each door. The house is bigger than she remembers; there are extra rooms that open into expansive chambers, undiscovered wings. *How did I not know this was here?* she asks again and again, elated, swimming expertly from room to secret room.

Then she hears a voice, garbled through the water, unintelligible, but calling out to her, urgent. She tries to swim upward, toward the voice, but hits the ceiling, realizing then that she's underwater, trapped. She starts to panic, kicking frantically toward the voice, now understanding *she's* the one in danger, and the voice is calling out to help *her*. The house seems dark now; she is down deep, far from the sun, frantic now, chest burning, trying to swim up and out of this house that had seemed like a home but is actually a cavernous tomb. Somehow she's swimming higher, through small hatches that open into new, vertical hallways. She strains to hear the voice, convinced that if she can, she will find the way out. What are those distorted, smothered words, tumbling through the water toward her, dissolving as soon as they touch her ears?

She can almost hear them now, the lost words, and there are shafts of light cutting through the water, through the sideways paneless windows—she is so close! But then she is falling, no longer ascending; something is pulling at her. She looks down, frantic, expecting to see something on her leg, some sea creature dragging her downward, but there's nothing—no, it's her own body, her own body turned to stone below the navel, legs heavy and dead as iron; she's sinking rapidly now, deeper into the house, which is no longer a house at all but a mouth, a yawning, jawless abyss open and pulsating and swallowing her whole.

Waking, breaking the surface of the sleep—she gasps for air, still panicky, the details of the dream already dissolving from consciousness, lingering only in her chest and limbs, heart hammering, legs kicking and flailing. Strange how the body remembers even as the mind forgets.

It is still night, no sign of morning. In the pitch black, veins coursing with dream-adrenaline, the fear she dismissed earlier returns, newly plausible: *There's someone in the house.* She had searched the master bedroom, yes, but not the rest of the house, only staggering blindly upstairs to collapse into bed. There are many other places someone could be hiding, many doors left unopened, corners still dark. The fact that she's been in her bed for hours and left unharmed is little comfort now that the fearful thought is chasing her, flitting around her head like a bat.

She closes her eyes, listens—the storm is waning; the wind has settled into a moan. The house is suffused with silence. This should comfort her, but it doesn't. The raging storm had made the house feel safer somehow, not invulnerable, but protective. But now, no longer united by a common adversary, the house seems to be colluding against her, its grim quiet conspiratorial.

If she cannot trust the house, there is nothing else to do but search it.

She begins in the room where she is, turning on the lights, calling out "Hello?" not expecting an answer—a part of her inwardly scoffing, in fact, at her irrational fear, her paranoid behavior—but the sound of her own voice cutting through the silence makes it smaller, more docile and ordinary.

She decides to work clockwise through the house, moving down the stairs, across the house, and up again. She will end her search at the door she would most like to keep closed, the door she hasn't opened in sixteen years, the door of the westward bedroom, once hers.

She moves methodically, hoping slow movements will calm her simmering fear, illuminating one quadrant of the house at a time. Each room, when exposed to the harsh and artificial light, shows itself to be blank and empty. *See?* the house seems to be saying to her. *Nothing to see here.*

Once she's resurfaced, shivering, from the freezing unfinished cellar, she goes back through the downstairs again, this time turning off the lights, no longer worried about what might be hidden in the dark. The dark, in fact, has lightened into a rosy gray. Dawn is coming. She will finish her search in the half-light.

She almost decides not to search the last room, her fear long since gone; she is motivated now by the reluctance to leave a task undone. And it's ridiculous, really, that she hasn't gone through this door since arriving here. It's just a room, after all, an ordinary room.

Two rooms, actually, one nested within the other, an inner sanctum. The bedroom door opens into the larger, longer room, while the inner chamber is to the left, through a doorless opening. As soon as she twists the doorknob and steps into her old rooms, she forgets why she entered, forgets entirely the search for a possible intruder, for the source of that felt but unseen presence. Why has she been so afraid? Why has she avoided opening this door? Now, once it's open, she's flooded not with fear but with wistful longing, the sweet pangs of nostalgia, a tenderness for the girl who once slept here, dreamed here. So many firsts. First sleepover; first garish attempts at applying makeup; first furtive sips of pilfered whiskey; first menses, an unexpected ambush. These are the memories swirling around her now like excited, impish pixies, each trying to catch her attention after having been long neglected.

The space is long and narrow, almost like a bowling lane, with a low peaked ceiling and single-hung windows at either end. The current owner has arranged the two sections as she once did, the outer chamber as boudoir, with a dresser, desk, bookshelves; the inner chamber as a sleeping space, large enough for only a bed and nightstand, a small rug. She is no taller than her teenaged self, but the room seems smaller somehow, the slanted ceiling closer, confining.

She walks through the open doorway into the bedroom area. There are two twin beds in here now, but once there had been just one, a bed where she'd first known the heat and light of another body, first succumbed to reckless, furtive desire. The first taste of what later, in college, would become perfunctory, a social nicety. Sex without love was a purely physical exercise; the body was touched but not the interior being, the core of the person, whatever that was that the ancients called the soul. But sex as love's expression, that was a different thing entirely, and she can still remember, still feel, the honeyed light of that October morning, the wordless communion, that feeling of being swept away, the self dissolving into sheer desire.

She remembers whispering to Cass, the next day, as soon as they crossed paths between classes: "We did it." *It.* Such a faceless, neutered word, as tiny and unappealing as an insect, a word far too inadequate to capture what had happened, which was more an event than an act. Even now, recalling the moment, she wants to reach for archaic, mythical language, *becoming one flesh.*

Cass had framed it as a loss, seeming somehow bereft, looking at her mournfully, incredulously. "You lost your virginity?"—sensing rightly that something had shifted, that her claim of friendship could not compete with a love that had been actualized in this way.

But did she lose something? That framing wasn't right either, too passive, too negative—and what was virginity anyway? Something physical? Immaterial? She imagines a gauzy veil blown away by the wind. But no, nothing was taken from her; she had made a free-will offering. And whatever she'd given away in this room, on that long-ago morning, whatever the name of that gift, she had wanted to give it for good.

She lies down on one of the beds, hands folded and tucked under her cheek, staring across at the empty twin. She imagines her teenage self lying there and pictures her asleep, at rest and full of bliss. Things had felt so *right* back then, when she had Adam, when they had each other. Why had she kept searching, then? Why had she abandoned the shore of that first, perfect love?

Her eyes drift closed; she can feel her body sinking into the bed, the room around her tunneling into black. Maybe she will sleep after all—then something, a sound, wrenches her awake. There's a rustling, no, a scraping sound, not random or frantic but deliberate, rhythmic, like a word being etched into wood. At first she thinks it must be an animal scrambling around on the roof, but the sound is not coming from the roof; it's coming from inside, from, or perhaps underneath, the wooden floor—and not close to her, but at the other end of the long, narrow room. It's coming from the closet, from behind the one door in the entire house she has not yet opened, and the thought of opening it, even touching the knob, fills her with dread.

She sits up, pulls her legs up to her chest, backing into the corner until the top of her head brushes the angled ceiling and her back is against the cold white wall, and she begins to shake her head, no, no. She closes her eyes, tightly, wanting to shut out all sensation, to retreat into an embryonic state; she is curled tightly into a ball. *No.*

There's someone at the door.

Her eyes flash open. There *is* someone at the door, the front door, and the sound of an engine, not a car, but—she moves to the window. A snowplow. There's a man plowing her driveway, someone she's never seen before. And the knocking at the door—it's Miguel. She recognizes his parka. He's standing on the porch, lightly tapping the snow from his boots between knocks, yelling and waving to the man in the plow. In the road, hazards flashing, is a tow truck loaded with her blue Fiat, which looks surprisingly unscathed.

She sighs, shakes her head. In the morning's white light, dazzlingly reflected by fresh snow, all the paranoia from the previous night seems like an awful joke. Night and solitude can do strange things to a person, not to mention hormones and troubled sleep. *You're such an idiot.*

She leaves the room hastily, glancing only once at the closet, which is mute and ordinary again. She is eager to thank Miguel and reclaim the car, knowing already where it will take her and what she must do, the thing she's been venturing toward, which has become inescapable.

It's time to find Adam.

Thirteen

The nursing home is right where it used to be, a short, squat gray rectangle, only one long corridor within, she remembers, the central vein from which leaf out about a dozen resident rooms, a cafeteria, and a common area. As she pulls up, looking at the building from the outside, the entrance flanked by heaping piles of freshly plowed snow, higher than the roof, she is reminded somehow of the crematorium she'd once toured at Auschwitz while studying abroad, a bunker-like building sunk low into the ground.

She'd spent some time in the nursing home as an adolescent, occasionally shadowing her mother's visits to patients there. She remembers one patient in particular: Alice with the dark ponytail that never turned gray, roving up and down the corridor anxiously in her wheelchair, right leg useless and bent up under her like a broken wing. Her limbs were sharp and scrawny, her eyes piercing, suspicious; she seemed more bird than human, but not in a fragile way—less sparrow than crow. Years later, when she first saw an ancient Greek rendering of a siren—that woman-faced creature with the spindly body of a bird, scaly feet—she thought of Alice.

"She was shot, you know," a nurse had told her, when Simone was helping her change the linens, getting ready to transfer Alice into her bed for the night. "By her husband." She gestured toward Alice, who was agitating in the doorway, rolling herself in and out, in and out. "That leg. You can still see the scar." Simone had searched for it as she wheeled Alice over beside the bed, peering at the bent-up leg and seeing a thick white circular scar just above the knee, still purpled at the center.

She was curious about Alice, the strange fire behind her eyes, her spiteful energy, her frenetic movements, so different from the other residents who ambled along slowly like cattle. Like most of the others, Alice had lost touch with reality—her words, when they came, were repetitive and nonsensical—but her senses seemed sharp, not dulled like the others'. Simone always had the feeling that Alice knew something, that there was some dark wisdom within her madness.

Once, for some forgotten reason, she'd been left alone with Alice; she remembers looking down at the bed, wondering whether Alice was asleep or awake or maybe even dead, and quick as fire Alice had whipped a clawlike hand to her throat, grabbing Simone's ball chain choker necklace with surprising strength, wrenching the girl's face close to her own, eyes flashing. "You let them in, they'll never leave," she growled, and Simone could feel the warmth of her foul breath. "You let it in; you let it in," she kept repeating, almost spitting the words, until Simone pried her fingers loose and jumped back.

Strange how this memory resurfaces with such force as Simone sits staring at the nursing home, still in her parked car. Strange how Alice springs forth so vividly from the depths, filed away long ago but somehow keeping herself whole, waiting to be conjured.

But perhaps there is a reason; perhaps Alice can help her out now, from the grave. After all, Simone can't just waltz in asking for Adam; she knows the speed and frenzy of the small-town rumor mill. What if he hears some woman is looking for him, without knowing it's her? (Surely if he *knew* . . .) She doesn't want him to be wary, on guard. She is instinctively secretive, already protective of this not-yet-rekindled love. Perhaps Alice is her ticket in.

"Can I help you?" The nurse at the reception desk stares at her blankly, and that absence of recognition, so wounding to Simone when she first arrived in Fall River, now feels like an asset, a cloak of invisibility.

"Yes, I'm looking for information about my great-aunt who used to be a resident here. I think she may have died here. I don't know her married name. She was estranged from the family. I promised my mother I'd ask about her while I was in town." The fibs tumble out of her.

The nurse stares at her suspiciously. Simone realizes with disappointment that of the two basic genres of nurses—the kind who care too much and the kind who care too little—this one appears to be of the latter, hardened and world-weary variety, succeeding long-term in the profession because she has long since ceased to empathize.

"She was your great-aunt. But you don't know her last name."

"It's a long story, and a weird story, I know." Simone's mind spins, searching for the likeliest lie. How old had Alice been sixteen years ago? Although it was difficult to gauge her age, she'd been younger than the other residents, addled before her time. She might have lasted another decade. "I think she died about five years ago. I understand if you can't help me."

"Do you at least know her first name?"

"Yes. Alice."

"Alice?" The nurse looks surprised. "And she died several years ago?"

"Yes."

"Well, look, I wasn't here five years ago. And there are privacy laws."

"I'm not looking for official records or anything. I was just curious if anyone here knew her, remembered her. Surely it's not illegal to remember someone?"

The nurse sighs heavily, an *I've got better things to do* sigh, and waves dismissively toward the common area. "You can try talking to some of the residents. They usually like visitors. I wouldn't get your hopes up, though. They might remember something from forty years ago, not sure about five."

Simone nods her thanks, and the nurse disappears into a back office. Simone lingers for a moment at the desk, pretending to sign in, scanning the walls for anything resembling a schedule, anything that might have Adam's name, eventually spotting a hanging clipboard that looks promising—but then the nurse is back, radiating annoyance, so Simone waves cheerily, a little too cheerily, and turns toward the common area.

The space is set up like a living room, centered around a large television nestled in an oak cabinet, attended by billowy recliners of varying colors, some of which are occupied. The television is playing an episode of *The Twilight Zone*, the original version; she can hear Rod Serling's tight-lipped narration murmuring over the scene of a frazzled middle-aged man in a convertible foraging in his pockets for a cigarette. She thinks of those Camel Blues and the silly wager she made yesterday, the result of which is still unknown—the thought is quick and fleeting, and she lets it scurry by.

Behind the recliners are two wooden dining tables, sturdy antiques, circled with mismatched wooden chairs and arrayed with half-finished puzzles. There's an old man wearing a red flannel shirt and suspenders at one of the tables; he's unbearded and bald, aside from a few ghostly wisps of hair floating up from the crown of his head. He's stretching out his right arm with sloth-like deliberation, trying to pick up one of those impossibly tiny pieces, fumbling a bit, but then he grasps the target between thumb and forefinger and places it somewhere in the middle of the unintelligible image where it snaps, miraculously, into place. A perfect fit.

He looks promising. Simone pulls up a chair next to the old man, whose drooping jowls give him an approachable, puppy-dog affect. From this angle, she can see that the puzzle's image is a photograph of one of the rose windows in Notre-Dame Cathedral. The puzzle has been worked from the center outward, an inner orb surrounded by eight smaller orbs, like a flower almost, but the disk much larger than the petals. At the center of the orb is the Virgin Mary in a robe of blue, the Christ child on her lap, and spinning out from this hub, a dazzling colored wheel with sixteen spokes, all but the first three half-finished, clockwise from Mary's crown. Each spoke, each long petal of the rose, ends in an orb with a human form inside, some saint or biblical figure she doesn't recognize.

She looks at the finished image on the box: a pattern of circular symmetry like a firework of colored glass, frozen at the instant of explosion, the flash of brightest light. Such intricate complexity, each ring of the rose, each tiny orb a mirror of the others, yet minutely distinct—how could this old man possibly see how the pieces fit together? She always approached puzzles like this from the edge inward, finishing the perimeter first, but he is working from the center.

She sits down next to him, feels suddenly shy, even though with him, as opposed to the nurse, she can safely ask truthful questions. "Hello. I'm Simone. What's your name?"

"Harold." He replies without even glancing at her, eyes still fixed on the puzzle.

"Harold," she repeats, looking where he's looking, her eyes following the languid motion of his arm, extending gradually toward a brightly colored tessera. He doesn't sift through the pile, doesn't even seem to pause or hesitate, somehow already knowing each piece and where it belongs.

"Do you like it here, Harold?" she asks.

"Here, Harold," he replies.

"You're doing such a good job with this puzzle." She's using her child voice, she realizes, the overly enthusiastic falsetto she slips into whenever speaking to the very young. "It's beautiful."

"Beautiful."

She leans closer, whispering now; she can smell the acrid puffs of breath coming from Harold's mouth. "Do you know Adam, Harold? Is there a nurse here named Adam?"

"Adam," he repeats, loudly enough that Simone glances around nervously to see whether anyone has heard. There's no nurse in sight, and the two white heads she can see poking over the edge of the recliners remain fixed on the television. The frazzled man on the screen is happier now, perched at the counter of a soda shop, apparently thrilled about his milkshake. No one seems to be looking at her, or even aware of her presence, not even Harold—except, there, in the corner, behind an overgrown fiddle-leaf fig tree, someone is watching. The face is hidden, but she can feel the heat of focused attention, a gaze trained toward her. She can see the wheels of the chair and two footrests, but only one bony leg extending down, bare below the knee; the other leg is tucked up, bent sideways under the body, sticking out like a wing.

It can't be.

Simone gets up slowly, circling back around the recliners to get a better look—and there, hiding in the shadow of the fig tree, is Alice. White-haired now, and hollow-cheeked, ancient as a crone, but very much alive.

And looking at her. Not just looking. *Seeing*. This is not the blank, absent stare of dementia, nor the vague haze of distant recollection; this is the sharp, piercing glare of recognition. Alice is looking at her, eyes tracking her every movement, mouth hanging open in a toothless, mocking grin. She lifts her right hand, fingers bent and gnarled into a claw, and she waves the claw toward Simone, two short strokes. *Come here.*

Simone ventures closer. Maybe Alice heard her ask about Adam; maybe she knows something. As Simone approaches, Alice begins to agitate, rocking back and forth in short, rapid movements; her mouth is moving now, shaping words without sound. Simone bends down, instinctively putting her hands on her neck, remembering the bite of the metal in her skin the last time she was this close to Alice. She's near enough to hear now, words so muted they are breathed rather than spoken: "Don't. Open. It."

Three words, then a strange, breathless, rattling sound coming up from her throat. Simone jumps back, glances anxiously around for a nurse, for help, then back down at Alice, who, she realizes now, is not choking but laughing. Laughing. Mouth gaping like a clown's, head tilted back, her crooked torso swaying in her chair.

Simone retreats, walking backward and hitting the corner of the television cabinet, which digs hard into her side; she turns, wincing, momentarily blocking the screen, but no one objects; the two bodies in the recliners are silent and still. Only Alice is moving. Only Alice is making noise, her winded cackling scored by despondent music from the television, the man onscreen hunched over and moaning in the dark beside a motionless carousel.

Then a nurse breezes into the room, cheery and portly in bright yellow scrubs patterned with cartoon cat heads, calling back over her shoulder, "I'll get him!" She makes straight for the tables, ringing out in a singsong stage voice, "HAIR-old, dear HAIR-old, it's time to go!" She releases the wheelchair brake with her foot and pulls Harold back from the table, his arm still hovering over the puzzle; a colored shard in between his fingers tumbles onto the floor as he's whisked back, turned.

"Go!" he yells, as if in protest. "Go!"

The nurse ignores him, calling out again to some unseen interlocutor. "I don't know. Adam is doing the evening shift. You can ask him." And then she's gone, sashaying down the hall with purpose, Harold slumped down in his chair, acquiescent.

Adam. The name is a charm that breaks whatever spell Alice had cast. Crazy old Alice, impossibly alive and mad as ever. Simone emits a forced laugh, as if to convince herself that Alice is nothing but a harmless fool, deserving of pity, yes, but certainly not fear. She shifts her attention to the information she's just been given, a gift from on high: Adam does indeed work here, and he will be here, in this building—perhaps this room!—this very evening. If this place still has standard shift hours, her mind churns quickly now, that means he should be done by ten.

She seizes this knowledge like a talisman, carrying it triumphantly out of the room, only distantly aware of Alice's quiet gasps of laughter and that voice from the television murmuring after her: "an errant wish, some wisp of memory ... some laughing ghosts that would cross a man's mind".

Fourteen

The man with the dark hair, thick dark beard, the man in the deep green parka. When he walks out of the nursing home—twin doors whooshing open, hushing closed behind him—at 9:31 P.M., she is there, waiting, keeping vigil in the parking lot. She's come early, unsure exactly when he'd be done. She can't just waltz in. Whatever it will be like, that first moment of recognition, it can't happen in *there*, that stale, sterile house of gradual dying, under the watching, mocking eye of Alice, or some top-heavy, disapproving nurse—no, this moment has to be carefully crafted. She has to bide her time.

It can't happen in a parking lot either, in the biting cold, faces half-masked by the dark. She isn't sure where, or even when, it will happen. She won't force it. *Don't force it.* Maybe not even tonight, although the thought is excruciating, now that she's watching him, just twenty feet away, alive and in the flesh—here! now!—not preserved in her memory like a wax figure, true-to-life but lifeless.

Part of her wants to gallop toward him, ambush him as he unlocks his truck—under the lamplight, by the piled snow, perhaps there is a certain romance. But she waits. No plans, no forethought, only pure, bottled-up expectation. She will know, as the moments unfold, what to do, and she will follow the breadcrumbs as they come.

She catches only a glimpse of his face, a quick profile as he walks through the sphere of the streetlight—but his walk, his pace, the arc of his shoulders, so familiar, and particular too, as distinct as fingerprints. She is seized by the sensation that she knows this man like she's never known anyone else. And been known by him in return.

What will be revealed in his eyes when he sees her, recognizes her? She will not be able to hide her longing, this much she knows. Will it be reciprocal? The same look mirrored in his eyes? Will he say her name? Will he need to? Or will what passes between them stay unspoken?

He starts his truck, lets the engine churn, warming up. Her engine is cold; she cut it as soon as she knew it was him—billowing steam from a tailpipe would be a dead giveaway. Her car is quiet, anonymous among the other cars in the lot; she's watching him in her rearview mirror. She's still warm inside her thick down coat, that enveloping blue, but she can feel the cold nibbling at the edges, at her fingers and toes, working its way in.

After a few minutes—heart hammering under her ribs like a small caged animal—she sees him pull slowly toward the main road. She waits to see which way he turns and follows, leaving her headlights off until she pulls onto the main road, an inconspicuous distance behind him. He's heading back into town, rather than continuing outward toward farmland. Maybe he lives in town now, in one of those residential rows that parallel Main Street. But he goes only a few blocks before pulling over and parking again—what's he doing? What could be open at this hour? Nothing but, yes, the bars. Those same two bars squaring off across from each other, somehow having reached a stable equilibrium, pulling roughly equally from a small pool of drinkers, regulars who committed to one or the other, and a few who straggled back and forth, sometimes on the same night: the Outlaw, on the north side of Main; the other called, with an air of resignation, Someplace Else.

He's parked his truck on the right side of the road, in front of the Outlaw. She watches him enter, then drives slowly past, pulling around the next corner onto a side street. She turns off the car and sits in the silent cold, watching her breath flow out of her like a phantom. She hasn't expected this. She was sure he'd drive straight home, that she'd see, at least, where he lived and then perhaps orchestrate a way to cross paths with him, sometime in the daylight, when they could see each other clearly, when she could have her responses refined and ready. *Simone, is that you? What are you doing here?*

But this ... a bar? Is a bar any better than a parking lot for the moment of reunion? Especially *this* bar? This sad, dank, small-town bar with a tacky Old West facade and fake saloon doors? A bar, moreover, that she's never been inside, that holds no memories; she left town years before she could legally enter. It will stink, she knows, with walls porous to decades of cigarette smoke and overturned beers; she hasn't been in this dive bar, but she's been in plenty. And this won't have the pumping energy of the college town bar scene, the dizzying, youthful din, disjointed conversations shouted over loud music. This will be a muted, disconsolate place.

And yet ... even as she sits there, she's already changing her mind. The half-light, the tacit anonymity, the ask-no-questions vibe of tired working men who just want to drink and be left alone—maybe it's perfect. She imagines Adam sitting at the bar by himself, drinking a beer after a long shift, completely unaware that someone from his past, not just *someone* but some past *love*, is about to step into his present, as from a portal through time, an unexpected messenger. She wishes she could experience that surprise and delight—will he be delighted?—she wishes she were him! But she is the messenger and, perhaps, the message as well. She knows she is coming but not how she will be received.

She knows she is coming. Yes, it is decided: This will be the night, the time, and the place. The damned Outlaw. In just two minutes, she will push through those saloon doors and then open the actual door behind them. She will feel the hot stench of old smoke and warm bodies and fresh booze on her face, and she will surrender to whatever comes next.

He is sitting at the bar, and he is by himself, just as she'd imagined, which she takes as confirmation that she knows him better than anyone, that their souls are still entwined. *Soul*. Normally, she would balk at the word, an academic reflex; her official position on the soul is that it does not exist, at least in a religious sense, in the sense of something real that needs *saving*, that is damnable. But the soul as metaphor, the soul as naming the unnameable force that seems to propel her forward, even now; the force behind each step through the small, sparsely occupied bar—whatever that was, that cord of desire, that primeval connection, a scientific term won't do. Here, one must reach for poetry and even, again only *metaphorically*, the numinous.

She imagines this—the entwined soul cord—as a visible, tangible, sinuous stream of light running from her body, from within her, from her *core*, and winding around and under the tables and barstools, which sit empty and askew, the only physical obstacles between her body and his, where the other end of this luminous cord terminates. She follows its imagined path and then she's there, just behind him, close enough to reach out and *touch him* if she wanted to, if she dared, but something stops her. She doesn't want to touch first; she wants to be seen.

She slides into the empty barstool next to him, face turned toward him expectantly—and, impossibly slowly, as if they are moving through water, he turns his face toward her, a face set in irritation at the disruption of his solitude, the sudden proximity of a stranger, an irritation that widens into confusion, disbelief, and then finally surprise.

"Simone?" At last, her name! But her name as a question, a question tinged with apprehension, even fear, a feeling she understands and knows—that fear that one's ordinary perceptions are no longer trustworthy, that the safe and measurable distance between *reality* and *self* has been breached, disrupted by something unexpected and unlikely. But is it ... unwelcome?

"Hi," she says, unable to keep a giddy, tipsy smile from playing across her face.

He turns his torso toward her while pushing his stool back a bit, a confused gesture of approach and retreat that she isn't sure how to read; he's scoffing but grinning at the same time, shaking his head, speechless.

"I don't understand. How are you here? I mean, what kind of booze are they serving?" He laughs and she can see the push-pull of trepidation and, yes, delight in his face, as he turns away from her, shakes his head, turns back for another look. Something in him is happy to see her; she can see it, and she fixates on that flicker, that spark.

"Well, you know, I never did cross the Outlaw off my bucket list."

He laughs, raises his glass, a tumbler half-full of whiskey. "I guess that's the downside of skipping town at seventeen."

She echoes his gesture with an empty hand, wanting to find that undercurrent of delight, tap into it, let it spill over and wash away whatever else is lurking between them, some kind of hidden sadness, some buried pain that has twinged at his words—*skipping town at seventeen*. Was that, perhaps, a subtle accusation? How had he felt when she'd gone? How exactly had they left things? She gropes momentarily for the memory of their last conversation, the last time they'd been close like this, exchanging words, but she isn't sure where they'd been or what had been said. Does he remember? Is there a buried subtext to his words?

"Here, let me help you out." For an instant she is pierced with a cold fear that he is somehow aware of what she is thinking and is about to reveal the opaque memory of their last encounter, and in that instant she knows, although she doesn't know *why*, that she doesn't want to talk or think about that time.

But no—he's responding to her words, not her thoughts, her lame crack about the bucket list; he's waving at the bartender to order her a drink.

"What is it these days? Surely not bottom-shelf lager. I assume we both got that out of our systems senior year. And don't tell me you're a Chardonnay girl."

She settles back into the banter, subduing the antsy fingers of her memory that want to keep sifting through the files.

"No way. I'll have what you're having."

He nods, pleased, makes a signal to the bartender, and before she knows it, she's sipping Jack Daniel's, neat.

"But really, what are you doing here?" he asks. "I mean, don't get me wrong; it's great to see you. But it's been, what, ten years?"

"Sixteen."

"Sixteen! You're right. Man, that makes me feel old."

He waits for her to take up his question, the obvious question, the first hurdle to any conversation she's had with anyone from here, from back then.

"To be honest," she starts, and realizes she genuinely *wants* to be honest, to disclose to him the secrets of her heart, at least as much as she can decipher—but how honest should she be? The precipitating reason doesn't really matter, and anyway, *that* whole situation is temporary, but maybe she can try to describe the rest. "To be honest, I don't really know. It was an impulse. This weird need to come back. I can't explain it, exactly. Like something's here that I've been running from, avoiding, but can't escape somehow.

Like I need closure, or something." She shrugs, feeling the protective heat of disclosure in her face, and looks away.

"I think I get it," he says. "I feel that way sometimes too. Even though I never left."

"Why didn't you? Leave, I mean?"

He sighs. "Well, I guess I did leave for a while, during college. Went to ISU. I didn't plan to come back exactly. I don't know what I planned. But then Dad got sick. I came back to help out, and then it just didn't seem possible to leave again."

Simone nods, sips her whiskey, eyes traveling over his face, at once so familiar, but also changed—a bit heavier, his beard thicker and graying around the chin, grooves around his mouth like parentheses. There is a sadness about him, a weight he's carrying; even when he smiles at her, his eyes teasing and playful, even then the weight is there.

"I still can't believe you're sitting here, talking to me." He shakes his head, looks away, the initial surprise settling into a kind of bashfulness. They keep doing this: looking at each other, then glancing away.

"I know," she says. "What are the chances we'd run into each other like this? Both in the same place on the same night."

There must have been something in her voice, some false note, that betrayed her. He looks at her again, newly skeptical but still amused, not hostile.

"Holy shit, you followed me, didn't you?" He's laughing now, a real laugh, his head thrown back. Simone is startled, unmasked, grasping for some lies that might cover her, lies substantial enough to cower behind, but the only ones she can find are too small and flimsy, capable of covering nothing.

He leans in and grabs her knee, still laughing, seemingly delighted. "You little psycho," he says, affectionately. The heat of the whiskey and this sudden exposure have dissolved any sense of distance or wariness between them; they've been drawn, just like that, into an erstwhile intimacy.

"How did you know where I worked?"

They are turned toward each other now, elbows resting on the bar, heads close, conspiratorial.

"Cass." Her face is flushed; she's embarrassed, but eagerly entering the rapport opened by her inadvertent confession. "I actually went there earlier today, to the nursing home, to see if maybe you were there, and I heard a nurse mention that you were working tonight. So ..." She shrugs. "I came back later and"—she smiles at him, guilty, but also brazen—"here we are."

"And here we are, what the hell." He laughs again and shakes his head, then raises his glass; she reciprocates, touching her glass to his, lifts it high, and with a rush of daring, tips the whiskey down her open throat, every drop, letting it run through her like fire, then slams down the empty glass, ready for another.

The other bodies in the room are mere shades, shadows, not real or substantial enough to disrupt the sense that *he* and *she* are the only two people in this cramped, dim room, perhaps the only two people in this town, in the whole godforsaken world.

They talk for over two hours, long enough for the bar to empty out, for the bartender to eye them with annoyance while polishing the glasses, wanting them to take the hint and move along so she can close up. "Last call," she says, harshly, when the clock finally tips in her favor. "Closing up in ten."

Adam nods, slides over his credit card, not giving Simone a chance to protest, to insist that she pay for her drinks—how many whiskeys? Two, three?

"So, where are you staying? The lodge?"

She shakes her head. "No, I rented my old house."
"You what?"
"Yeah, it's a vacation rental now."
"That's insane. You're insane," he says, but he's looking at her with something like awe. Neither of them wants to leave, she realizes. In here, they can pretend that time is a loop, a circle, rather than a ruthless line. But out there, just beyond the fake saloon doors, is the real world, cold and harsh and indifferent to old love.

"I drive past that house sometimes. Hasn't changed much."

"Yeah, it's been weird to be there, honestly. I think it's messing with my head a bit." She wants to add, *spending too much time alone*, but that's too overt, too brash.

"You okay to drive?" he asks. "That's a few miles out there."

She nods. "I'll be fine."

They are standing now, putting on their coats, walking toward the door, not speaking; she waves once to the bartender, who does not wave back. He pauses to let her through the doors first, and then they are outside, facing each other. The night is clear and deeply cold, windless, the snowpack on the sidewalk and the street glowing in the light from a waxing moon.

"It's been good to see you." He says this quietly, not as a platitude, but a confession.

"Yes," she says, waiting.

"How long are you in town?"

"A few more days."

He hesitates. They are on the threshold of something. Neither wants to walk away, yet neither wants to be the first to cross it. "Where'd you park?"

"Around the corner."

They turn and fall into step together; he's walking her to her car; it's the gentlemanly thing to do.

"*That's* what you're driving?" he says when he sees the Fiat. "I don't think I've ever seen an actual Fiat in Fall River. That tin can isn't gonna cut it out here."

"I know," she says, "I'm an idiot. I rented it back in Portland. I didn't think."

"Look, let me follow you home. It's a calm night, but there could be ice. Would hate for you to end up in a ditch."

"No, no, you don't need to do that. I'll be fine. I'll drive slow."

"Simone." His hand is on her arm, gentle but firm. "It's happening. Get in."

Her heart is in her throat the entire drive back to the house, her eyes flicking back and forth from the white road ahead to the headlights in the rearview mirror, as if the twin lights from behind her are somehow holding her, carrying her safely along, as if she is no longer driving herself at all.

The truck matches her, mile for mile, turn for turn, until she can see the peaked roof cresting on the rise, the driveway approaching. What will happen then? Will the headlights continue straight ahead, passing off into the night? Or will they turn in behind her, pull close?

She turns into the driveway, the house dark and mute yet somehow staring, watching the scene with suspense. The truck turns too, lumbering into the recently plowed drive behind her, then stopping, idling, long enough for her to think, *he's parking, he's getting out, he wants to come in*—but then the two lights are steadily retreating, backing toward the road, swinging around to face the opposite direction, pointed toward town. The brights flick on and off once, twice—a signal, a farewell—and she watches as the taillights, narrow and red like snake eyes, fade into the night.

All at once a cold comes over her, an isolating chill. She trudges toward the house with resignation, with disappointment, and even, yes, relief. But underneath it all the certainty, the pledge, that this will not be an end but a beginning.

She's thinking about a moment back at the Outlaw, not long after she'd downed that first whiskey, when he'd briefly turned away from her, fumbling with his coat, which was slung over the back of the barstool. He'd angled his body in a strange way, as if trying to hide something from her, but she'd caught a glimpse anyway, a quick flash of metal on the fourth finger of his left hand, just before the hand disappeared into a pocket, then reappeared, bare skinned.

Fifteen

That night, her dreams are full of Peter. An irony: After days of ruminating about Adam, reveling in carefully curated memories, willing their reunion into existence, actively pushing away all thoughts of Oregon, of Peter, of their life together, of her current *situation*, the *predicament* that she came here to quietly and secretly resolve but is instead actively avoiding—as if denying something can make it unreal—after days of evasion it all finds her, cornering her in the only place she is docile and unarmored: sleep.

They are in Oregon in spring, when everything erupts in bloom, when the gray tunnel of winter rain recedes, when earth and sky yield to the sun again and all the buds open. There's a month, maybe, a handful of weeks, when there's a balance between rain and sun, a sweet interlude between the unremitting deluge of winter and the pitiless summer heat, which scorches the grass. They are in this interlude, there, together, on the warm grass, surrounded by billowing hydrangeas, heavy with round, dripping blossoms. They are reclining, face-to-face, caught in a shared gaze that is both given and received, free from self-consciousness and unease, the kind of gaze that, in the waking world, is too intense to be sustained and breaks quickly into withdrawal, self-protection. No words pass between them, only some other silent language, the language of gesture and sign. The earth itself seems to be breathing, and they are caught up in the rhythm of its undulating breath.

She feels a sense of fullness, in her heart, yes, but also her body—*her body!* It's expanding, ballooning, her torso curving out into an orb before her very eyes. How can this be? She is curious, unafraid, expectant. And, beginning with her navel, her belly begins to bloom into the blood-soft petals of a rose. She is opening, unfurling.

"Oh!" she says, with surprise and delight, looking over to Peter, knowing his face will mirror back her joy, which is truly *their* joy—but instead of delight she finds horror, he's looking at her in terror, mouth frozen in a soundless scream, and she looks where he's looking, back down at her body, but instead of a rose there is a gaping hole, a crater; she's hollowed out, and whatever form had held those petals intact, giving them shape, has been dissolved; the blood is everywhere, all over her, viscous and formless. She tries to scream but, like Peter, no sound comes, there is absolutely no sound; even Peter is gone now, vanished, and she is utterly alone, more alone than she has ever been.

She wakes long enough to feel the ache—the yawning, devouring ache. Eyes still closed, she presses her hands against her abdomen, surprised to find skin rather than an open pit; how carved out she still feels, empty and hollow, too much to stay awake, so she lets herself be pulled back under, back into sleep.

Peter again, on the end of the couch, the other end from where she sits, under a lamp, open book in her lap, a thick, hardbound novel. Her legs are stretched out, her feet resting in Peter's lap; he's holding one of her feet in his hands, kneading the arch tenderly like dough. He's asking her something, but she's not listening; his words are muffled and fuzzy, unintelligible. She's not listening because she is searching for something, searching in the book, flipping through the pages, engrossed in this novel, a love story, that she can't put down but that also can't be read—the letters jumble themselves around when she tries to focus on a word. She has to finish the story, has to know the ending, but she can't read the words on the page.

Some of Peter's words reach her; he is telling a story too, a story that happened to him that day, a stranger who came to his woodshop, asking for a casket, a small, handmade casket, small enough for a child, an infant actually, a stillborn baby. She wants to listen to him, but she can't pull her attention away from the book she's trying to read, the story she must finish, that has her entranced. Her hands are spread flat on the page, fingers outstretched as if trying to make the words lie still, long enough for her eyes to capture them; but as she stares, the letters begin to sprout, long thin tendrils erupt from the words and wrap themselves around her fingers, tightening, cutting into her skin. Just like that, her hands are tied, tangled in knots, the threads as sharp and strong as fishing line.

She wakes again, this time wrenching her eyes open and half sitting up, fighting against the undertow, forcing herself to stay awake, flexing her hands and fingers, which are mercifully free. "Bloody hell," she whispers, exhausted but unwilling to undergo another round of dreams just yet.

She turns on the bedside lamp, sorting through the images, which are already beginning to dissolve—what lingers longest is the feeling of Peter's hands on her feet, his long fingers, his touch, both gentle and strong. The story he was telling in the dream is a true one. Two years ago, not long after they started dating, she had dropped by his shop, a small garage he rented, where he did his solo woodworking projects. This artisanal carpentry work was a side business; it wasn't big enough to pay the bills and all but went dormant during heavy construction season, when he was busy with contracted work. But during the slow pace of winter, when he had more freedom, he would take on smaller custom projects, working on a single piece for weeks at a time.

It was early evening, and deep winter, because it was already pitch-black outside. Peter worked by lamplight, three or four lamps scattered around the small space, each emitting a golden glow. He never turned on the fluorescent ceiling lights, which gave him headaches and, he said, blanched the color of the wood. He tried to work with natural light, during the day, but that evening he was working late. A woman had called him, he said. He didn't know her, but she went to his mother's parish. She called and said that her daughter, who'd just gotten married in June, had given birth to a stillborn baby at sixteen weeks. She wanted him to make a casket, but the funeral was soon, the day after tomorrow. Could he make something in time? So there he was, working on this tiny wooden box.

"They're having a funeral?" she remembers saying, then feeling embarrassed at the incredulity in her voice. "I didn't know people did that kind of thing." And as she watched him work, she felt an inner tension, a confusion around how she felt about this situation—and more so how she *should* feel. Because she did feel an instinctive pang at the word *stillborn*; her heart sank and she felt that tremor one feels at the news of a tragedy, the sense that something dark has passed close by, alighting on someone else's house, but also the sense that it could just as easily have visited her, and perhaps would, next time. But just behind this wave of pity and dread—a wave that seemed to push her *toward* the tragedy, *toward* the grieving mother she didn't even know—there quickly came a second instinct, a dubious skepticism, a distancing, a retreat. Sixteen weeks isn't very far along. Barely out of the first trimester, well before any hope of viability outside the womb. She knew these technical details at least, courtesy of her physician mother. But other details, she realized, were unclear. Would it even look like a baby at this point, or like one of those weird fish creatures? She knew the heart started beating early, if those awful pro-life billboards could be trusted, but did that matter? What about the brain, consciousness? Was it even aware of anything at this stage? It had died, technically speaking, but had it ever really *lived*?

These were the questions running through her mind as she watched Peter work, watched him sand smooth the small casket, each measured stroke bringing out the natural grain, like some buried treasure surfacing from the depths. The casket was so tiny; she had seen a child's casket once before, the son of a colleague who'd died at the age of three—that had been awful, she shuddered just remembering the pallbearers, only two, carrying the short casket on their shoulders—but this was almost comically small, like it was being made not for an actual person but for a toy funeral home; it was a doll's casket, absurd.

It was clear to her that Peter had none of these questions churning through his mind as he worked; he was enveloped in the work of his hands, in bringing forth something of beauty and dignity from dead, dried wood.

And he did. When she saw the final product the next day—Peter had worked through the night—she gasped at its delicacy, at the glowing red cedar panels set in a frame of light-colored pine; no staining, just oil, to bring out the natural beauty of the wood, the grains that looped like concentric oval rivers, or like sound waves echoing out from a central galaxy-shaped knot. She picked it up; she could hold the entire thing across the palms of her hands.

Peter brought it to the parents himself. He gave it to the father, who answered the door. When Peter told her about it later, his voice got rough; he had to stop talking, mid-sentence, and in that moment, in the gap between his words, his tender sorrow entered her, and she realized that she could love this man, that perhaps she already did.

The dream had uncovered this memory in her; it surfaced like the wood grain, her conscious preoccupations sanded away. She feels a longing for Peter's steady presence, to share with him everything about her strange and surreal visit here, everything; even—how unthinkable!—her rendezvous with Adam that night. What would it be like to lay it all bare, all her desires and fears, her dreamlike missteps, her erratic behavior—and most of all to speak aloud the secret that drove her here, the secret now, at this very moment, quickening in her womb, its heartbeat fast as a hummingbird, its bean-like body suspended, burgeoning, buoyant in a watery orb, concealed behind the veil of her flesh, but no less real for that. What would she say to him, if he were here right now? How would she tell it?

O red fruit, ivory, fine timbers!
Boarded the train there's no getting off.

Sixteen

Of course, there *is* a way off the train. It's in her suitcase right now. She brought it with her, intending for this trip to be the moment of disembarkation. But perhaps the truth of the poem is that there is no *easy* way off, no detraining without cost; there is a process unfolding within her that can be interrupted only by an act of violence—toward herself, toward *it*—however small.

Violence. She contests the thought as soon as she thinks it; that's the wrong word. What she has in a small packet, inside a white paper bag, buried in her suitcase, is therapeutic, medicinal. At this stage—her best guess is nine weeks; there'd been no ultrasound, or even a pelvic exam, just a urine test and a short conversation—there is no *baby*, not even a *fetus*, only an embryo. She pictures it like a seed that has just barely sprouted, the husk splitting open to show a hint of green, but no actual plant yet, nothing with roots. "You're just bringing your body back to baseline," the doctor had said.

Two medicines: one larger, round and white, taken orally; the other, a handful of hexagons, inserted directly into her body. The first arrests the pregnancy; the second empties the womb. It would all be over in a matter of hours—assuming all goes well. Assuming she doesn't hemorrhage, or get an infection, or ... she had not closely read the litany of possible complications. "Safe and effective," the doctor had assured her, repeating those twin words several times like a mantra. She'd heard her mother use the same ones many times.

As soon as she *knew*, as soon as the existence of the burgeoning sprout was known, she had the urge to flee—and she hadn't known right away; after all, she took her pill every morning, as she had since she was fifteen. Pregnancy was a distant, unlikely threat, like cancer. She'd had a very light period that cycle, just some spotting really, but that sometimes happened on the Pill. It's not a real period, her mother had told her when she first wrote the prescription years ago—just "withdrawal bleeding." What did that mean, anyway? All these things her mother said in passing, but never fully explained; she accepted them without asking for more information, assuming, perhaps, that she didn't need to know.

So menses could not be a true messenger for her; it was a tamed creature, subdued into an artificial rhythm, a simulacrum. What clued her in to the quiet revolution in her womb was the hunger—the ravenous midmorning *need* to eat a full meal well before lunch. She remembers sitting at a coffee shop back in Portland, clicking away on her laptop; she'd had a cappuccino, as was her habit, and normally she wouldn't eat until after noon, skipping breakfast altogether. But that morning, right around ten o'clock, she was suddenly—there's no other word for it—*ravenous*. Someone had ordered an omelette, and the smell of fried eggs and crisp, greasy ham overcame her, possessed her; her craving was predatory, rapacious. This was the first sign that her body was waking up in some strange new way.

She took a drugstore test that day, and the second pink line popped immediately, darker than the control; she didn't need a three-minute wait.

That was when she began to withdraw, retreat. First, in small ways, spending more time alone, not asking for entrance into Peter's private world—*What are you thinking about? How was your day?* And when he knocked, with either words or touch, she kept the door closed tight, hiding behind excuses: headaches, fatigue.

Even teaching became unbearable—standing up and speaking in front of all these expressionless faces, feeling herself on display, as if her hidden condition was somehow detectable, as if their impassivity was only a guise for disgust. How grotesque would it be to let the thing play out over an entire semester, to balloon before their very eyes—their youthful, inscrutable eyes—like some freakish science experiment. Luckily it was already finals week; after a few painful days she could retreat fully into hiding, mind already racing about how to *take care of it* without Peter knowing anything.

Why did she hide it from him? Again, this was instinctive. In retrospect, she can only speculate about the hidden, animating reasons. Perhaps because she wanted privacy—that's what *Roe* was all about, after all, the right to privacy. But that's just another way of restating the question—*why* the felt need to keep it completely private, breaking the silence to not a single soul, not even her collaborator, her co-creator.

The hiddenness, the secrecy, made it less real. If this could all go away quietly—*back to baseline*—it would remain unreal, like something that *almost* happened. If she was the only one who knew, her own gradual forgetting could erase the existence of this ... *situation* entirely, correcting the timeline of her life. There was this, and also the fact that she *knew* Peter; she knew without asking that he would want to keep it, and the disagreement would be so deep it might just break them. This way was cleaner, even merciful; this way, he would never feel the loss.

Safe. Effective.

So she decided from the beginning (decided without deciding, the reasons ex post facto) to keep it hidden, toying with the prospect of going away somewhere, but hating the idea of a *hotel*—imagine, bleeding alone under a mass-produced, soulless print in a bed that had held hundreds of strange bodies—and then her mother had called, she'd found the house online, and as soon as she saw it, she knew where she needed to go. It seemed inevitable, a magnetic pull. Only now, when the time of execution is at hand, does the plan seem rash and somewhat ill-advised. If everything goes smoothly, it will be a success. But if something goes wrong ... (*Safe*, she reminds herself, *effective*.)

But nothing has been like she expected since returning to Fall River, to the house; she had not been prepared for the eruption of the past into the present, the reopening of a road not taken. She came here with the intention of quietly repairing a rupture in her life, a secure, successful life that she had carefully curated, steadily ticking off goals one by one: doctorate, tenure-track job, relationship—and motherhood was not on that list, at least not yet.

But now, something else is calling to her, something else is beckoning. Instead of closing that rupture and restoring the equilibrium of her comfortable life, she is tempted—consumed—by the thought of abandoning it altogether.

What if everything my mother told me was a lie? She's sitting in the dark, alone and full-grown, yet this transgressive thought runs through her with a shiver. She lets herself think it, heart hammering. What if the good life is the small-town life? The mother-wife life? The homemaking life?

Don't get married young. Don't have kids before grad school. Don't give up your career. (That there would be grad school and a career was a given.) Such were her mother's rules, instilled in her from a young age, and she'd followed them dutifully, never questioning—until Adam.

She now has two motives, two compelling reasons to do what she came here to do. But the reasons conflict: The same choice, the same act, opens two possible trajectories—one back to the secure and successful life with

Peter that she left in Oregon, and one that goes back even further, full circle, to the small, rooted life she left first, a life with Adam.

In this moment, alone and afraid, she feels a longing for maternal comfort and guidance. A memory surfaces from when she was little, maybe ten, when she was first going to Cass' house for a sleepover. Cass' dad, Bruce, was there to pick her up, his truck idling in the driveway. She climbed in the back, heart fluttering with excitement—she and Cass had been anticipating this moment all day, talking breathlessly at recess, making plans. But as she sat there, watching her mother and Bruce talking on the porch, the engine began to feel less like a hum and more like a growl. She imagined the moment when her mother would go back inside the house and the door would close and Bruce would walk back toward the truck and climb inside and the truck would start to move and there would be a stretch of long minutes alone with him and she'd never been alone that long with a grown-up man in her entire life—and before she knew it, she'd flung off the buckle, she was out of the truck and scurrying to duck behind the garage, in the tall weeds, waiting for what seemed like forever while they called her name, hiding until she heard the heavy tires crunch against the gravel and the growl of the engine fade away and finally: silence. Only then did she come out, seeing at once her mother's dark silhouette on the porch, arms folded, only guessing at the shrouded expression on her face, expecting hard anger, exasperation—but then seeing instead, as she walked closer, curious concern. "Where were you?" Cynthia asked, more bewildered than accusatory, and at this unexpected tenderness Simone had burst into tears, unable to explain, but somehow her mother understood anyway, pulling her close so she could cry against the soft flesh of her belly. "Don't cry, sweetheart. You never have to go with a man anywhere if you don't want to. It's okay to run if your body says run. Remember that."

And Simone had. She'd remembered it in college, when her roommate stooped into the dark recesses of a Volkswagen van, tipsy and bumping her head as she did, tumbling against the jumble of legs within, arms reaching out to grab her, steady her—limbs belonging to a group of guys they'd met at the bar who were going down to the beach to party, limbs beckoning to her from the darkness, disembodied hands and voices ushering, "Come on, come on!" But something had halted her, some inner force surfacing to issue a single, forceful command: *Don't*. And she obeyed.

She'd remembered it other times too, whenever a *no* would rise up in her chest, unbidden, as if there were an oracle buried deep in the well of her body, asleep until some threat made the oracle flash awake and climb up out of that well, eyes blazing.

What would the oracle say about her current predicament? she wonders, closing her eyes to listen, the room so quiet she can hear the soft hush of her breath and the settling of the walls, as if she and the house are breathing in unison. But underneath this, silence. The oracle is quiet, sleeping at the bottom of the well.

Her mind drifts back to that moment on the porch, which feels less like a memory and more like something that is happening now, as if she could walk downstairs and out the front door and step right into it, embracing both her mother and her child-self at once. She feels a piercing ache, a longing to call her mother and show her this turmoil, this wild tangle of choice and desire, to have her mother become omnipotent again, larger than life, and somehow undo the knots.

But she also knows that her mother would answer with the voice of a doctor, not a mother, and she knows what that voice would say, because she has heard it before.

Her mind pulls toward that memory, that awful day, but she quickly redirects, letting it drift instead toward the woman whose presence, after so many years, still somehow pervades this house.

Cynthia was a woman of two lives. Simone imagines these lives like tapestries, thick fabric scrolls etched with images—one displayed openly, hung high on the wall, adorned with the stories that everyone was allowed to know, the stories she's heard again and again, carefully curated for public consumption. She knows this one well.

Cynthia. Lone daughter of an alcoholic from Nowhere, Ohio—some forgotten copper notch in the rust belt. Taught herself how to read. Taught herself how to drive. Squirreled away every cent she made until she could afford to buy a jalopy and Get Out. Woke up early one morning while her father slept off a bender and drove west until she saw mountains—and never looked back. Put herself through college, top of her class. Put herself through medical school. Started a surgical residency, then switched to family medicine. At some point in this era—"Med School"—Simone came along, and then there were two lives on the tapestry, interwoven, Simone strapped like a papoose to Cynthia's back as they roamed around the West—New Mexico, Utah, Wyoming, then Idaho. Cynthia always preferred to be on the move, taking short-term stints in high-need remote areas, as if forever reliving that first morning break toward freedom at seventeen, racing away from a collapsing, corrosive past into a seemingly infinite expanse. This is the clearest image she has of her mother's past, which isn't even her memory, but a memory passed down: a grim-faced teenager with straggly straw hair, hands white-tight around the wheel, backlit by the rising sun, in perpetual flight.

The only clear characters on this tapestry are Cynthia and Simone—the rest are wraiths that never fully materialize and disappear quickly from the story. Cynthia's father, wifeless and nameless, factory worker by day, drinker by night, until the factory shut down altogether and he could drink full-time. Not a violent drunk, as far as she can glean, but mute and glazed over. Cynthia's mother, a fun-loving, promiscuous waitress, whisking through the story like a tumbleweed, only around long enough to give birth and skip town. Are they alive or dead? Simone doesn't know. They are as unreal to her as characters in a fairy tale. They are stories told to her, nothing more. And yet they'd shaped her life because they'd shaped Cynthia's, and Simone was strapped to her back, along for the ride.

Until Idaho, until this house, they were always on the move, changing jobs and towns on a semiannual basis. Cynthia became a doctor not because she liked science, or because she liked people (she didn't particularly like people), but so she'd never be poor, never trapped in one place, never without options, never stuck in a failing industry, never like her father. Birth, sickness, and death are the only constants, she'd say, and she didn't want to be an undertaker. And there were always small, isolated places in need of a doctor—middle-of-nowhere places. Cynthia had a taste for the godforsaken.

These are the familiar, well-told stories—exhibited openly, but also disconnected from one another, episodic. There are gaps of months, sometimes many years—each blank space like a mouth opening to form a question.

The answers to those unasked questions are hidden in her mother's other life, a tapestry that is rolled up tight and locked away. Simone has never seen this tapestry in full, has only caught glimpses of what is concealed there, brief sketches—just enough to awaken but never satiate her curiosity.

Enclosed in this second tapestry, for example, are the exact circumstances of Simone's birth. What she knows about her father can fit in one hand, a meager collection of crumbs she's gathered over the years as Cynthia has dropped them one by one. They "dated" in med school—Cynthia said the word contemptuously, as if it were a euphemism for something terrible. They were both in the same competitive, top-tier surgical residency in the Pacific Northwest. Cynthia got pregnant and took a leave of absence from the program, eventually giving up on the surgeon track altogether. But he stayed, waiving his parental rights before Simone was even born. That's all she knew about him—that he was out there somewhere, that he was a surgeon, and that he'd never wanted anything to do with her.

There was another mystery that shrouded her coming-to-be: Why had Cynthia decided to keep her? This was a perennial question, arising at regular intervals, especially when Simone was a teenager and spending more time helping out at the clinic. Several times, she witnessed the same scenario: Cynthia's female patients turning up with unplanned pregnancies, even though Cynthia herself had prescribed them birth control. Sometimes these were young, naïve teens, perhaps a little fuzzy on the birds and bees, but often they were adult women, many of whom already had children and were thus well aware of the causes and realities of pregnancy. Cynthia found this perplexing, exasperating, often muttering to herself after the patient left, "Why does this keep happening? They're on birth control. This shouldn't be happening."

The clinic was small, with thin walls, and a number of times Simone had overheard her mother's conversation with a pregnant patient. Cynthia's first question was usually the same: "Was this planned?" If the woman said no, and especially if she was unmarried, or already had two or more children, Cynthia would gently offer to discuss "options", that is, the various means of termination. But sometimes the woman would refuse from the outset, shaking her head vigorously. "Nope, I'm keeping it." Simone, highly attuned to even the most minute shifts in her mother's moods, would glance at Cynthia's face as she exited the room after these encounters, notice the corners of her mouth pull downward and her lips purse. Reading the disapproval on her mother's face, disapproval that was tinged with disgust, Simone would feel a sense of vertigo and the recurring question about her own origin would arise. Her mother clearly thought that abortion was the best choice for these women, yet this was a choice she had not made for herself when she'd been young and single and fallen pregnant at the worst possible time. In these moments, Simone would feel a harrowing mix of relief and disquiet, as if she'd narrowly missed getting hit by a bus.

Once, and only once, she had heard her mother admit to one of her patients that she'd had two abortions herself. The patient was sitting on the bed, her face in her hands, rocking softly back and forth saying, "I don't know; I just don't know." The door to the exam room was partly open; Simone had been passing by in the hallway and slowed down enough to observe the scene, to hear her mother say in a low voice, "I know it seems like you'll never get over this, but you will. I've had two myself."

This revelation shocked her—not the abortions per se, routine procedures that, after Simone's time in the clinic, had become banal, but rather the disclosure of a reality that almost was, the prospect of their small dyadic world pried open and disrupted by additional personalities. These might-have-been siblings, their ghostly forms now emerging, barely visible, on the hidden tapestry, but where? When had this been? Before her or after? And why had she been chosen, but not the others?

Cynthia revealed this part of her past to her patients, but never to Simone, not even when, not long after this eavesdropping, she'd come to her mother with a newly discovered burden to confess. She mumbled the news shakily, waiting for Cynthia to comfort her, to say to her, *I've been there too, and it will all be alright.* But she'd just stared at her, coldly, her face a rigid mask. "You should have known better. You of all people."

But no, that is not something Simone wants to think about, not tonight. She shakes her head, scattering the memories that are crowding around her like gnats, shooing them away. None of that matters anymore. Some things are best tucked away, left to fade. Perhaps she, too, has a hidden life. Perhaps this is inevitable, the culling of recollections, separating out what we choose to remember, and what we prefer to forget.

Sleep is coming for her now. She can feel it cresting like a dark wave, offering escape from both the present and the past, and she welcomes it.

Seventeen

She sleeps late, waking up groggy and dull headed, hungover from one too many whiskeys and far too much sleep. It's late in the morning already, maybe even noon. She can tell by the hazy sunlight suffusing both windows equally, rather than slanting in through one end of the room, bright and angular.

Meeting Adam at the bar—had that been just yesterday? It feels long ago already, on the far side of an interminable night of dreams and rumination, memories boiling and rising to the surface, so vivid and poignant that she feels as if she's had visitations from both Peter and her mother, whose presences linger; perhaps one of them could be downstairs now, making coffee. Peter would grind the beans fresh— she closes her eyes, imagining—timing the water just right, on the cusp of a boil but not quite. She teases him about that, his scrupulous precision, but she loves his coffee, would kill for a cup right now.

She presses her fingers against pulsating temples. Adam. Peter. Cynthia. Three planetary bodies whirling around her, each exerting a gravitational pull, herself a small moon, maybe an asteroid, pinging among them, dizzy and overpowered.

Each new day in Fall River greets her with a crossroads, divergent paths stretching out before her and disappearing over the horizon into separate fates. The longer she's here, the more paths there seem to be, and she has come to loathe the burden of choosing. She wants to be chosen.

The first choice before her is a small one, but with potentially weighty consequences. On the drive to Idaho, once the mapping app had guided her to roads she already knew, Simone had let her phone die entirely, later tucking it in the bottom of her suitcase, next to the white paper bag from the pharmacy, which is where both items still sit, inert but potent, like little bombs that could be activated at any time.

Last night, after the dregs of the final whiskey, Adam had asked, "How long are you in town?" She had answered honestly. "I'm not sure." In reply he said nothing, but slid his napkin toward her, placing on top of it the pen he had used to sign for the check. Slowly, as if moving through water, she had picked up the pen and etched the nine digits of her phone number on the napkin, sliding it back without a word. He folded it twice, into a little square, then tucked it into the inner breast pocket of his parka. The exchange had felt intimate and conspiratorial, like two undercover agents trading classified information, quiet and careful, in case they were being watched. But who would be watching?

Since coming to Fall River, she had ignored her lifeless phone instinctively, a way of shielding and separating herself from her present life, with all its entanglements, in order to come here and do what she had planned to do. She'd been afraid, especially, of Peter's voice, his gentle, guileless voice, the one thing that might erode her resolve.

Secondarily, she was also avoiding Cynthia's intermittent texts and calls, which, for reasons that were less clear, now felt intrusive. Ever since embarking on this trip, Simone had been beset with conflicted impulses regarding her mother: both a pining for her and a compulsion to hide from her.

But now, to continue evading Peter and Cynthia also means evading Adam. She considers whether that might be best, whether she should recommit to her initial strategy of hunkering down and shedding her burden alone, in secret, then reentering her life, unscathed. Once she returns, once she is herself again, Peter will forgive this short interval of silence. *I was immersed in my work*, she will say, a condition he knows well.

But Adam—being with him, feeling their long-dormant passion begin to awaken, the chemistry, the familiarity, as if no years at all had passed, as if time had folded back on itself in that dingy bar, as if they had permission to be young and heedless again. A door had opened last night, and they are standing on the threshold. Will they walk through it? *Should* they? Is there a difference?

Of course, it is not entirely up to her. She made the first move, orchestrating the encounter, but now she is in a passive position; he has her number, not the reverse. And now he can decide to either reach out again or ghost her. She can't tell which scenario she hopes will unfold; her desire is strong but conflicted and unwieldy, like a monster with too many mouths, a dozen tongues lashing out to taste a dozen things. Does she want *drama* or *safety*? *Romance* or *stability*? She isn't sure. Both prospects yield a rush of anxiety. She can't be sure what she will choose, but one thing is clear: She needs to know what *he* will choose, either way.

She swings her legs onto the cold hardwood floor and walks over to her suitcase, which is splayed out on top of the dresser, disheveled, but still packed. Digging down under her folded jeans, she fumbles for her phone, fingertips grazing the white paper bag, but letting it be.

She pulls out her phone and lets it rest in her hands, surprisingly weighty, a dark mirror through which she can see her distorted reflection. She plugs it in behind the nightstand, waiting a minute or two before pressing the power button, then backs away to a perch near the foot of the bed to watch and wait.

After a quiet interval of gradual reanimation, her phone suddenly erupts, buzzing and pinging and dancing with light and color like a miniature slot machine. She watches it with growing dread, watches the alerts pile onto the screen, one after another, texts and voicemails and unread emails, names blinking by: Peter, yes, several times, and Cynthia, and also her next-door neighbor, the doctor's office, her department chair, and several students, no doubt appealing hastily calculated grades—and oh no, even the dean ...

After a minute or two the deluge is over; her phone lies as dark and motionless as a corpse after the cessation of final convulsions.

She has observed the digital maelstrom warily, with both anticipation and dread, watching for a message from an unknown number, but none has appeared. Perhaps, in the stark light of day, last night now seems foolish to Adam, the sparks between them fueled by whiskey, the door best kept shut. Yet she is surprised at the force of her own disappointment; she had expected—wanted?—to feel more relief amid the tumult of emotions, some part of her ready to accept the sign that one of her possible fates now lies behind a closed door.

A sudden, shrill sound cuts through the stillness, so loud and insistent that at first Simone fails to recognize it: the landline phone, directly beneath her, in the kitchen, ringing. After a moment of frozen confusion, Simone jumps up and rushes down the stairs, suddenly frantic to answer the phone before it stops, even as she's remembering that this is not actually her house, that no one would be calling her at this number, she hasn't given it to anyone, but maybe Adam knows the number anyway, somehow; he knows she's staying here—

She grabs the receiver. "Hello?"

"Hello? Simone?" Not Adam. A woman.

"Yes?"

"It's Cass."

Cass, that's right—Simone had called her from this landline; she would have the number. How many times had she stood in this exact spot, with a similar receiver pressed to her ear, listening to those same words? "Hey, it's Cass." Back then, she'd switch quickly to the cordless to escape Cynthia's hearing—so sharp and ranging, like a bat's—and scurry off to the privacy of her room to have another absurd, rambling conversation that would last late into the night, fizzling out only as they each dozed off, the line still hanging open.

It is not yet six o'clock in the evening, but already pitch-black outside, the windows of the house dark like open mouths, revealing nothing of the outside world; they might as well have been in a submarine or floating in space. The curtains are flung open, and Simone has a brief urge to close them, feeling exposed—how easy it would be to see inside the brightly lit house—before remembering there is not another house, another soul, around for miles.

"It's so dark already." She says this much out loud to Cass, who is sitting across from her in the living room, wine glass in hand, askew in a puffy, oversized armchair that dwarfs Cass' slight frame. It is strange how much Cass still looks like herself—herself from *before*—lean and athletic, petite, red-gold hair in a long bob, large and angular eyes, cat eyes. And that same alert, nervous, feline energy, as if she could dart away at a moment's notice, impossibly fast and totally silent.

"Solstice," Cass replies. "Shortest day of the year."

"Oh shit, you're right!" Simone lifts her glass. "Lo Saturnalia."

"I have no idea what that means, but okay." Cass mirrors Simone's gesture, and they drink. They have downed a bottle already and are starting a second, a heavy Italian red.

Simone sips her glass slowly, wanting to maintain the pleasant, floating feeling that has blossomed in her head and is now gliding through her body. "This was a good idea," she says.

"Well, it was either this or meeting up at Bud's for a head-sized hamburger. Not a lot of options in Fall River."

Cass had arrived about an hour ago, bearing a cardboard box heaped with cartons of Indian takeout, which she'd packed in from the next biggish town over, thirty miles away. Simone had supplied the wine, selecting one bottle from the local market, hesitating, then taking two more—a decision she does not yet regret. Each glass of wine seems to slough off several years, bringing them back to the fast friendship they once had, that intense, adolescent intimacy. They had talked casually through dinner, reminiscing and laughing about the past, its brighter, comical sides, nimbly avoiding the dark. But now, having retired to the living room and popped the second bottle, Simone can feel it—they are on the edge of deeper disclosure. But she doesn't want to go first.

"Okay, I have to ask." Simone leans forward, lowering her voice, letting her tone become more serious. "What's the deal with your parents? Why were you so freaked out that I went to their house?"

Cass exhales forcefully, glances in the other room, as if someone else might be listening. "What do you remember about my dad?"

Simone shrugs. "I don't know. I mean, he was funny. Pretty gregarious. Kind of a scary driver. Remember when he drove us to Jackson Hole that time? For the track meet? I swear he straddled the median the entire way down the mountain." She shudders. "I was terrified. All those curves."

Cass doesn't respond, apparently waiting for Simone to go on.

"He was at all your games, I remember that. And every single meet. To be honest ..." She hesitates. "I was a little jealous. That you had a father who came to your games. Not like, crazy jealous or anything. I didn't resent you. I just wondered what that would be like. I wished I had that, you know." There is a heavy pause, a fleeting sadness that ripples across Cass' face—or is it pity?

Simone wants to keep talking, to turn the conversation back toward Cass and break the onerous silence. She reaches, rifling for recollections. "I did see him lose it that one time, with the umpire of the softball game. I can't remember what set him off, or even where the game was. It was an away game. The umpire was this woman, probably fresh out of college. I mean, she was young. He walked around the dugout and onto the field. You remember this?"

Cass stares at her blankly.

"Your dad got in her face. I mean, he screamed at her. His face got all ... He just lost it." She sits quietly for a moment, caught by the image of Cass' father, his red, contorted face, a mask of pure rage, his arm raised high—a memory she hasn't summoned in a long, long time, and quickly it pings another memory, one that surfaced just the night before, a memory from further back, when, faced with the prospect of a car ride alone with him, Simone had fled and hid.

"Cass—"

"I don't remember that." Cass is staring down at her hands. "But I can picture it. Because that's how he was at home. He would fly into these rages, turn into this other person. Sometimes ..." Cass stops, looks up at Simone. Her eyes are wide and luminous, deep green pools, but her voice is steady. She always had the ability to cry without crying, like water seeping from a buried spring. "Sometimes it got really bad. I'd sleep in the basement, just to be farther away at night. That helped a little. If he needed to hit something, someone, being out of reach was good. But other times, he'd find me anyway."

"Holy shit," breathes Simone, flailing around for the right words. "I had no idea."

"Yeah. I don't know, it's weird. When you're young, it's like you get used to the really awful things that happen at home. You think they are normal, or that they won't affect you, or that everyone's parents are like this. But when you get older and suddenly see everything the way it actually was, it's like ... It's like your whole past, your whole childhood, has been wearing this mask, this *clown* mask, and you peel it off and there's a monster underneath." Cass stops, takes a long drink from her glass, emptying it. Simone gently pushes the bottle across the coffee table toward her.

"And it sucks because there were good times too," Cass goes on, tipping more wine into her glass and swirling it absently. "There's real love mixed in. And then it's hard to tell the difference. What's the real love and what's the counterfeit, you know?" She takes another drink. "But once I saw it for what it really was, I had to get out. I had to leave it all behind—the house, them, Fall River, everyone. It was all twisted up together."

Cass sets down her glass, stares hard at Simone. "There's a darkness here, in this place, this town," she says, a strange urgency gathering in her voice. "Some people seem to like it. Some people choose to stay. That's the kind of darkness it is. A darkness people choose."

Simone wants to say something, wants Cass to explain—her words have tripped something deep within her—but she is also confused, resistant. She doesn't understand. She sets her glass down, feeling that the conversation has taken a turn into something unpredictable, disconcerting, a half-tamed animal that is no longer caged.

"I mean, don't you feel it, Simone?" Cass looks around her, gesturing at the walls, the furniture. She has not raised her voice, but there is a fevered energy building in her tone, her body. The air is tensile, as if the house itself is listening in, trained on their every word. "Isn't it weird to be back here? Isn't it hard? It's weird for me, and I didn't even live here. I mean, this was never my house." She shudders, looks at the bared and blackened windows. Simone follows her gaze, seeing only the room reflected, their staring faces.

"Look." Cass directs her attention back toward Simone. "There's a reason I called you today. A reason I came. I don't think you realize—I haven't been back in over five years. I never thought I'd come back at all, but I had to come and warn you."

"Warn me?" Simone is beginning to feel dizzy, lopsided.

"I had this dream, Simone. About you. The same dream for three nights in a row. The first night, the first couple of nights, I thought—whatever, just a weird dream. I figured seeing you again would dig up all kinds of things. But the third night ..." She shakes her head, closes her eyes. Her voice drops to a whisper. "And it's weird because," she hesitates, "I'm not totally sure it *was* a dream. I mean, I'm calling it a dream because I don't want to sound like a crazy person, but—Simone, I swear I was *awake*."

"What was the dream?" Simone is surprised to hear an undertone of impatience in her voice, realizing then that she doesn't want to hear any more. She wants Cass to leave. She wants to be alone.

"I saw you, here, in this house. In your old bedroom. The one up there." Cass points at the ceiling, her voice dropping to a whisper. "Right above us."

Simone looks up at the textured ceiling, with its shadowy terrain of minuscule valleys and small, sharp peaks, haphazard and patternless. She continues listening to Cass while scanning the random lines and ridges for some kind of image to emerge, a word, or maybe a face.

"You're there, standing by the closet, and you look lost and just, so *alone*, like this little orphan. And there's a woman standing there. I can't see her face, because her back is toward me, but she's veiled. She has on this long veil. And she's holding something in one of her arms. I can't see what, but she's cradling something in her left arm, like she's holding a baby. And her other arm is stretched out toward you, like this, like she wants you to come to her."

Simone shrugs, forces a laugh. "That doesn't sound so bad."

Cass sighs, pressing her lips in frustration. "I know. It doesn't." She laughs dryly. "I actually—well, I have this friend, or at least this woman I know, in my yoga class. Anyway, she does readings. Like tarot cards, that kind of thing. I was so freaked out after the third night, the third dream, that I told her about it."

"What did she say?"

Cass looks down, as if reluctant to answer. "She ... well, she said it was a good omen. An omen of rebirth and healing. She said she knew who it was—not *what*, but *who*; I remember she said that. She said she knew who it was and that *she*—she called it *she*—is a loving mother, like a totally loving mother, nonjudgmental, totally affirming. She doesn't worry about good or evil, right or wrong; she just wants you to be happy. You can ask her for anything, go to her for anything, and she'll say yes to what you want, no matter what." Cass shrugs. "At least that's what she said."

"But you don't believe her?"

Cass leans back against the chair, closes her eyes. "All I know is that in the dream I'm screaming, and I'm screaming *no*. I'm doing everything I can to stop you, to keep you from going to her. That's when I wake up. Or whatever. I hear myself screaming *no*."

Simone says nothing. This is not what she had expected. She had wanted to confide in Cass, to tell her about Adam, about her predicament, to hear her commiseration, her advice. She had longed for the old Cass, Cass the best friend, the kindred spirit, the confidante. But that was not the Cass she got. She realizes now that it was foolish, cruel perhaps, to have expected the years to just curl up and disappear, as if nothing has changed. They are different people now, clearly, inhabiting different worlds, and this new Cass frightens her. There is a strange look in her eyes, otherworldly, unstable. The only thing she wants from Cass right now is for the conversation to end.

"Look, forget it. It's stupid." Cass, perceptive as always, can see that Simone is bothered, antsy, looking to extract herself. She stands up. "It's late. I should go."

"No, no ..." Simone gives a half-hearted, perfunctory protest, even as she stands and turns toward the door.

Cass lifts her heavy coat from the chair, and they exchange meaningless parting pleasantries, a few final apologetic reassurances: "I'm sorry, I don't usually drink this much."—"Don't worry about it. It's been so good to see you."—"Yes, let's keep in touch. Text me before you leave town."

Simone opens the front door, feeling a pang as she hugs Cass for what she suspects is the last time. The cold air swirls into the house around them, enveloping them, then rushing between them as they part.

Cass steps through the door, then turns back. "I know this is probably just all my own shit, and I'm projecting it onto you, but—" She steps forward, grabbing Simone's arm, looking at her with those angled, knowing eyes, pleading. "Don't you remember how bad it got? At the end? Before you left?"

Simone pulls her arm slowly back, forcing a faint smile. "I mean, of course I remember." Her voice sounds artificial, like a recording. "I remember that time well."

Cass looks into Simone's eyes, searching for something that she evidently does not find. "There's remembering, and then there's really *seeing*, you know?"

Simone does not reply, holding her tight smile intact as Cass turns away once more and steps beyond the sphere of the porch light, disappearing into the dark.

Simone, shivering with cold, feeling numb and exposed in her thin cotton cardigan, closes the door with relief. Instinctively, she turns the dead bolt, hearing it slide into place with a conclusive, gratifying *click*.

Eighteen

Simone moves quickly through the downstairs rooms, flicking off the lights. One by one the rooms darken, and as they do, the world outside pops back into perception. The black mirrors in the walls become transparent once again. Despite the cloud cover—for days she hasn't seen more than a streak of passing color in the sky—there's some kind of dull light suffusing the terrain.

She pauses in the downstairs bedroom—Cynthia's—as the room goes dark and the outlines of scattered trees and sloping stretches of snow faintly emerge. She moves closer to the window, which a moment ago had seemed menacing, a harsh barricade, but now transmits the only light source seeping into the room—what is that light? Where is it coming from? There are no outdoor floodlights, no streetlamps on these rural roads. The clouds are too thick to reveal any stars, and the moon is nowhere to be seen.

She walks slowly up the stairs, stumbling a bit, not tipsy but tired—densely tired, lead-tired, her body a millstone she must drag up to bed. Is it beginning? The physical signs that her body has been taken over, co-opted by an autonomic process? Why does it have to be so *hard*, the drudgery of generating new life? She thinks of the sprouted husk, the ruptured seed, so tiny and inconsequential, yet soon, if steps aren't taken, she will feel its cataclysmic presence throughout her whole body.

At the top of the stairs she turns left without thinking, shuffling numbly into the western bedroom, her old room, the room she's mostly been avoiding. Apparently now her defenses are down. Her aversion is gone. The room is calling to her, as if in soft lullaby, and she is already half asleep as she lets herself fall onto the bed.

There's a moment in the middle of the night when she almost awakens, hovering just under the surface of sleep, enough to be aware that she is in the old house, in her old bedroom, that it is winter, the longest night of the year, that dawn is still hours away and she shouldn't wake up, shouldn't open her eyes, shouldn't move any part of her body from under the warm shell of the blanket, lest the stimulus of cold air and half-lit shadows wrest her fully awake and leave her stranded there.

She fights to stay asleep, fights by pushing away from her senses, those portals to the waking world, resists by plunging away from reality and diving instead after the vanishing remnants of whatever she'd just been dreaming. She knows that if she can grasp some lingering image, a fragment large enough, it will pull her like an anchor, a deadweight, back into insensible dreams.

She manages to escape every sense but sound. Her hearing is too acute, too alert, her ears already trained on a faint but repetitive sound approaching steadily from the opposite end of the long room. Footsteps. The original fir floors, beautiful yet distressed by time and use—they protest when trod upon, weakly enough to escape notice in the activity of daytime, but in the silence of night, the sound carries, unmistakable.

Simone knows this sound, the groan of footsteps on fir floors. As a teenager she learned to close her eyes and just by listening pinpoint her mother's precise location in the house by her familiar, shuffling step, a sound eerily similar to the one approaching her now, though heavier than her mother's, and slower—not a shuffle but a measured, deliberate stride.

Her body is alert now with whatever sense is able to intuit another's presence, discern that one is no longer alone. Yet she keeps her eyes closed, holding on to the chance that sleep will reclaim her. How much she has come to crave sleep since coming here, not a sleep turbulent with dreams, dreams too tangled up with the real world to be restful, but the blank spaces between the dreams, intervals of pure slumber, absolute forgetting, when the body is allowed to relinquish all anxiety and desire. She knows this happens, because when she is able to enter that kind of sleep, there is a moment, just as waking is unfolding, when she is aware of this whole-body amnesia, a half second of pure present, before the body remembers again and the swells of grief or fear or longing return, followed quickly by conscious recollection and, often, rumination. Ironic that this feels like real freedom—not the ability to choose, to foist one's will upon the world, but instead the fleeting instant when the vicissitudes of life are suspended and there are no choices to be made. Yet *she* is still there, her self intact, able to experience this ephemeral bliss.

But that is not where she is right now. She is conscious and already weighing her options: to ignore the sound and feign sleep or to open her eyes, sit up, and look.

She looks.

She sees nothing, at least nothing out of the ordinary, nothing beyond the contours of the vanity and, behind it, the profile of the closet door, which, she is relieved to note, remains shut. Nothing moving, nothing out of place.

Yet the sound continues, unmistakable, so clear that Simone can approximate the distance of whatever is making the sound, a distance that diminishes with each step. There—it's next to the vanity. There—a foot closer, in front of the door to the hall. And there—it's standing in the inner archway, the opening between the two chambers, only six, five feet away now, approaching—yet still, she sees nothing.

An impulse, a shot of courage, and she's flung back the covers, she's out of the bed, her bare feet pressed against the cold floor, rushing toward the sound, arms out in defense or defiance, she's unsure what she is doing, what impulse is driving her. She moves quickly, lunging through the archway easily; there is nothing to stop her, nothing of any density or weight, nothing but empty air—but *cold*, suddenly, *cold*—a sheet, a veil of freezing air just beyond the archway, she hurtles through it like it's a pane of invisible ice, gasping with the shock of it, the jolt to her senses, the nerves in her skin on fire, having moved through a cold so bitter it burns.

"What? What?" she hears herself exclaim, in surprise and alarm, on the other side now of whatever that passing sensation had been. She's looking back through the archway and into the inner room, toward the disheveled bed where she'd just been lying. There is no sound now besides the agitations of her body, her hammering heart, her rapid breath, her own steps edging backward.

She whips her arm out and pulls it back, lightning fast, as if testing the voltage of an electric fence. Nothing. No change in temperature, no unseen subzero curtain. She runs her hands over her face, her arms, a soothing gesture, but also searching, as if her skin is a corroborating witness and can verify what she's just perceived.

She rushes back toward the bed, feeling instinctively that it is still the safest place in the room, part of her aware, embarrassed, that she is behaving like a frightened child, but relieved nonetheless, *so* relieved, to reach the bed, to burrow under the heavy down comforter, which still holds her body heat, to let its warmth soothe her.

She closes her eyes. Not to sleep, but to draw inward, to listen vigilantly, and also to hide. *I need to get out of here.* The thought rises up. *I need to get out of this house, this haunted, godforsaken house, and never come back.* Eyes still closed, she sees herself: huddled and terrified in the corner of the room where she slept as a girl, a place she'd left so long ago, and yet somehow never left at all. What is she doing here? What hormonal madness had possessed her, driven her through hundreds of desolate, snow-lined miles back to this house full of ghosts?

Out of nowhere, she thinks of Alice's leering face, her mad cackle, her enigmatic warning. What was it she had said?

Her eyes flash open. There is something, someone, at the foot of the bed. Looming up from the floor, a woman—or at least the form of a woman, shrouded by long dark hair or perhaps a veil—a hooded, feminine shape, face hidden in shadow.

As she stares at it—at her?—transfixed, she feels something akin to recognition, and a warm daze settles over her, a languid relaxation, like the kind of lethargy one feels on a stifling summer afternoon, a glazed torpor—yet here in the dead of winter. Her mind feels blank, vacant, like a drawer that has been emptied out. Distantly, she hears a sound, a single clear chime.

Look, the shadow-woman seems to say, without sound.

Slowly, as if moving through water, Simone turns her head to the left and sees a dome of pale blue light. She reaches toward it mechanically, realizing as she does that it's her phone, lit up by an incoming message. She is aware of the shadow-woman there in her periphery, watching her pick up the phone, watching her read the words sent at three A.M. from an unknown local number, only six words, six short words: *Hey, it's Adam. Are you awake?*

As she reads them again, letting the words and their meaning sink home, she turns her eyes back to the foot of the bed, seeing nothing there now except a bare, deserted wall but hearing, not too far away, the slow creak of well-worn hinges, the sound of a door closing—or, perhaps, swinging open.

Nineteen

The snow is so deep that the fences are buried. Every so often she can see the top of a post peeking out from the surface, like a hockey puck lying on the ground. Along the roads there are yellow poles, tall, about six feet high, that mark the edges of the road once blizzard season comes, once the storms roll in and drifts form, shifting the contours of the terrain, burying visible markers. Without these snow poles, the drifting snow could disguise the existence of a road entirely, erasing it from sight altogether, blurring and burying the lines that, in summertime, seem so clear.

They are nowhere near the roads now, no snow poles in sight, and it's been a while since she's seen a protruding fence post, or any man-made thing. Except, of course, the thing they are riding, the snowmobile, the sleek roaring engine underneath them, sliding and bucking over the snow, a swift metallic beast.

He had ridden right up to the front porch the next morning, telling her ahead of time only that he was picking her up and to dress for cold weather. She layered a sweater on top of several shirts, some leggings under her thickest pair of jeans—all her clothes flimsy and inadequate, but perhaps piled together would do the trick. And on top, her thick blue down coat, which she'd come to see as a trusty companion. She laced her boots as tight as she could, and with three pairs of socks on, they actually felt like they almost fit. Still, when completely clad and sweating in the living room, waiting by the front door, overly punctual, she felt like a plump caterpillar with cartoonishly large feet.

She expected to see his truck when she heard the sound of an engine and stepped out eagerly onto the porch—but there he was in the front yard on a jet-black snowmobile, the visor on his helmet flipped up, his eyes sparking up at her, relishing her surprise.

"Saddle up," he said, holding out a helmet, a mantis head to place atop her roly-poly body.

They set out on the old railroad grade, the remnants of a defunct branch of the Union Pacific Railroad, tracks long since torn out, leaving a wide trail—dirt and gravel in the summer, snowpack in winter—that started east of town and extended for miles, all the way into Wyoming.

This is how they began, on a named and well-groomed trail, crossing an old trellis bridge over the river, the town's namesake, stopping there to watch, in silence, the water rush underneath them, too fast to freeze, before they continued on, farther from town, from all the towns, and toward the distant peaks.

At some point—to Simone it seemed sudden, accustomed as she'd become to the contours of the trail, familiar and secure—Adam took an unexpected turn. The terrain had flattened out, the trail almost flush with the surrounding landscape, distinguishable only by the grooves left by previous fellow travelers. It was here that Adam took a hard left, veering off the trail entirely into open land, cutting across a wide sprawling meadow edged by evergreen forests.

Since then, they have been in the wild, crossing over a land without boundaries, without limits, flying along without a map, steered only, she assumes, by instinct and memory. Whose land is this? Who knows. *Trespass* has no meaning here. If there are any signs, they are buried under the snow.

Once, just once, soon after he'd turned, she'd thought of asking Adam whether he knew where he was going, but she'd have had to shout the words to be heard, probably more than once, and it seemed easier just to lean against him, to let him lead, to let herself be carried along, to watch the trees blur together, the miles beneath them disappearing in plumes of snow.

She is aware, vaguely—cued by that slight but shrill part of her that seems always on alert for possible danger—that if something happens to Adam, if the snow machine flips, if he becomes unconscious or worse, she would have no idea where they are, no idea how to get back or where to look for help. She would be lost. She *is* lost, already, reliant wholly on Adam.

This fear, small but potent, like a mosquito whine in her ear, is all but drowned out by a clamor of desire, not simply for Adam—although there is some of that, pressed against him as she is, arms wrapped around his chest—but a more capacious, yawning desire for the wildness around her to impress itself upon her, to disclose its secrets, to pry open the closed orb of her mind and crack her world like an egg, open.

A little fear, then, and this gaping, looming, nameless desire—and yet, underneath this turbulence, a heavy, torpid feeling, a honeyed thickness that she's felt since last night, since seeing or dreaming the woman in her room.

How paradoxical, her current state—reckless with longing, yet weighed down, dazed. Maybe it is the snowmobile, everything moving too fast.

Whether by coincidence or some second sense, as soon as she thinks this—*We're moving too fast*—Adam begins to slow down, steering them toward the line of trees, toward a cluster of lodgepole pines jutting upward, tall and straight, silent guardians. Amid the trees, as they approach, she can see the rounded, bare surface of a boulder, submerged save for the very top, which stretches out like a stone blanket thrown upon the snow.

He pulls right up to the rock and cuts the engine, then stands, stretches, steps onto the hard surface, turning to extend a hand to help her down from their steel-skinned mount. She leaps onto the rock beside him, pulling off her helmet and feeling, with relief, the rush of cold, fresh air over her skin; she gulps it in, out of breath, as if she's been running, realizing, now that she's relaxed, the quiet exertion of tensing her muscles for what might have been an hour.

Everything about the surrounding landscape dwarfs them—the expansive fields of white; the sharp-peaked mountains that have grown steadily larger, which loom somehow, though still at a distance; the rigid, silent trees, wary of their sudden presence; even the boulder on which they now stand, whose hidden height and weight she can feel beneath her. They are the outliers here, tiny and hasty, rushing from one place to another, searching for something to give meaning to their short, rushed, grasping lives—while all around them, these quiet, patient witnesses watch and wait.

"Pretty, huh?"

It is strange—how much she's longed to be alone with him, but here, in this setting, she craves solitude; the land around her seems poised to form a question, and she wishes she were alone to face its silent interrogation.

"Thirsty?" Adam, who'd been digging through the saddlebags, has turned and is offering her a thermos.

She takes it mutely, her eyes and ears still trained on the encircling landscape, caught up in its daunting beauty, and when the hot liquid pours past her lips, down her throat, it burns, making her choke and sputter. "Ugh," she cries out, pitching forward, letting the liquid pour from her mouth onto the snow, which it pierces with brown-tinged holes, like acid eating through skin.

"Hot? Or too much whiskey?"

Simone, still bent, tests her tongue against her teeth, confirming from the few taste buds that aren't scorched that she's just swigged a mouthful of hot—blistering hot— toddy. She can feel the trail of heat down her neck and past her heart, settling into her stomach.

"Geez. I thought that was just water." She hands the thermos back to Adam.

"Gotta stay warm out here. Inside and out. It's beautiful and all, but the cold can sneak up on you quick, and before you know it, you feel all warm and sleepy, like you just want to curl up and take a nap right there in the snow. And that's, well, that's when you die." He takes a cautious sip from the thermos.

"Do you know where we are?" she asks. She's still looking outward, eyes roving the vastness, but whatever spell it had been casting on her—whatever call she'd been about to hear—is gone. The beauty is still there, but muted, flattened, pointing only to itself, a postcard beauty.

"More or less."

Simone is disappointed, and somewhat ashamed, to realize that she is annoyed at Adam. His presence feels cumbersome, intrusive—no longer the steady, reassuring, masculine presence she'd leaned against as they sped here. She'd felt and enjoyed the presence of his body, but now that he is talking, here is not just a body, but another mind, another consciousness revealing itself, intruding upon her own.

Adam crouches down, gingerly sitting back on the rock and extending his legs outward, sighing contentedly. He is wearing a full-body snowsuit, black with yellow angled stripes under the arms and across the chest, wasplike, an impression accentuated by his broad shoulders and narrow hips. He'd always been tall and lean and still is, even if thicker, sturdier now. Studying him, looking at the line of his jaw as he leans back his head, closing his eyes and holding his face horizontal to the sky, she feels a glimmer of tenderness and desire return. She sits down beside him, her coat swishing beneath her.

"That's quite a coat you got there," Adam says, without opening his eyes. She wonders whether he's having a moment like she had just a bit ago—a taste of the sublime. She realizes she does not have a clear sense of Adam's inner life; their singular, first-love passion had been a wordless, bodily communion—deep and intense, but never quite reaching or disclosing the inner mysteries. There is more here to experience, she realizes with eagerness, more to uncover. Adam is a land not yet fully mapped.

"I know." She laughs. "I bought it at the thrift shop on Main. I don't own a heavy coat anymore."

"Boots too?"

"Yep."

"Can leave 'em with me when you go back. Looks like they might fit." He's looking at her now, teasing, a smile playing in his eyes. But his words, *when you go back*, hang between them awkwardly, lingering with unexpected weight. *Does he notice?* she wonders. *Does he feel it too?* Does he hear that door opening, that pathway to another life, a second chance, perhaps? Or is this just a day trip to the past for him?

"What's it been like, being here?" he asks. She listens hard for subtext, for a question underneath the question.

"It's been ..." she starts, stopping when she realizes she is unsure how to respond, whether she wants to offer a simple, small-talk answer—*It's been good!*—or attempt to gather all her disparate emotions and experiences into words. *Good, weird, hard, scary, painful, exciting, confusing.* All the adjectives fall uselessly like pebbles through snow.

"Exhilarating," she says finally, testing him with this word, gauging his reaction.

"Wow, *exhilarating*, huh?" He repeats the word, drawing out the syllables. "Last I heard you thought this place was pretty boring. What was the phrase you used? From that poem you were always quoting? 'This decayed hole among the mountains.'"

"Really? I said that?"

"Yessir, and not just once. That was your favorite thing to say about Fall River. Back then anyway." He pauses, and his voice softens. "You couldn't wait to get out of here then. You shot outta town like a horse on fire."

She waits, unsure what to say, aware now of a soft red thread of pain in his words, not hardened, but still tender.

"Did I?" she asks, after a moment.

"Yeah." He laughs, and she can hear a bitter edge to it. "Don't you remember?"

Does she? When she thinks about that time, her mind gathers and reports back a series of facts, a synopsis. She remembers that time like she remembers the basic plot of a novel she once read. But the *color* of that time has been washed out. The report comes to her in gray typescript, like newsprint.

"I remember being excited about going to college," she says.

Adam shakes his head. "No, you were more excited about leaving than going anywhere." He waits a moment, studying his boots. "I mean, do you remember that last winter? How it all went down? And then our moms went apeshit and, hell, I thought they were gonna kill each other. I mean, us too, but ..."

Until this moment, until the words *that last winter*, she had been curious about his version of the past, wanting to pry and hear more about his recollections, how he perceived her, how he remembered their love. But abruptly, at *that last winter*, her curiosity takes a sharp turn toward dread and she wants him to stop talking. Now.

She grabs the thermos out of his hands. "This cool enough to drink yet?" She takes a swig, then another, feeling it burn, but not from heat—just the whiskey burn, that sweet burn.

"Whoa there! I don't want to have to carry you back." He grabs the thermos, but he's laughing too, the smile in his eyes again, and he takes a drink.

"Maybe"—he edges closer to her, barely perceptible, but she feels it—"maybe we should go back to *exhilarating*."

It's an invitation. He's leaned back on his elbows, and his face is upturned once more, not to the sky but to her, his lips apart. It's an invitation, and she accepts.

Twenty

It is the voice that wakes her. A hoarse, rasping voice, coming from the opposite end of the outer room—not speaking, exactly, not making words, at least not that she can decipher. The sounds are like imitations of words, muted and drawn out in a simulacrum of singing, but the notes never arrange themselves into a discernible melody.

She opens her eyes fully, moves her legs and arms on the bed, expecting to be frozen in some kind of sleep paralysis, that half-awake dream state, but her body moves freely and her eyes are wide open and she still hears the wordless, rustling voice.

She sits up, peering into the darkness of the outer chamber, and as she does, she hears another sound—a rhythmic wooden creak, like someone stepping on a floorboard, but over and over again at the same interval, in the same place.

There's something by the closet door. A figure, barely discernible, a moving shadow, sitting in a chair that couldn't possibly be there: Cynthia's rocking chair. She knows that chair; it held her many times, especially as a little girl when Cynthia would read to her at night. She knows it well but hasn't seen it in years, assuming it must have been sloughed off in one of the many moves, like most things, Cynthia always downsizing, divesting herself of possessions, living now in a furnished apartment amid strangers' things.

Nonetheless, the chair is here, tilting back and forth, and someone is making it move.

She blinks her eyes, straining to see in the dark. The figure in the chair is angular, yet appears to flow down and over the back and arms of the chair like something liquid, yet holding its shape, not like a person at all—except ... No, it is a person, a person wearing a long, fluid veil that spills over the sides of the rocking chair, over the subtle protrusion of a bent elbow resting on the chair's right arm, bent as if holding something.

She ventures closer, enthralled, a cold knot of terror in her belly while her mind nudges her forward, retrieving what Cass' medium had said: *She's loving, all-embracing, there is no good or evil in her eyes, you can ask for anything, she longs to say yes to anything you ask.*

Closer now, she can discern additional movement from whatever is resting in her arms—surely an infant, what else would be cradled, nestled, held close in this way? There's something stirring against the veil—or is it a shroud?—a small leg perhaps, gently kicking? But the movements are so smooth, liquid almost, sinuous, like a wave rippling up the edge of the shroud as it hangs over the chair.

The voice is now making a chittering sound, the veiled head drooping low, and Simone swears she can hear faint words hidden in the sounds, words that remind her of a bizarre lecture she once heard while studying abroad, a disheveled old British professor talking animatedly about witches in the early modern period and their familiars, spirits who took the form of small animals, willing to favor the witch in exchange for an offering of some kind—milk or bread or blood. One witch that he described in particular—this is the part she never forgot—would summon her familiar, a ferret named Bid, with a little chant and then suckle him from her breast, feeding him with her own body's milk. "Come Bid, come Bid, come Bid," she'd call. "Come suck, come suck, come suck"—emphasis heavy on the second words: *Bid, bid, bid. Suck, suck, suck.* Simone swears she can hear those words now, or something like them, in the raspy, chittering voice—but surely she is imagining them? Surely this is a dream, a random compilation of distant and recent memory? The lecture from years ago, the conversation with Cass, all tangled up now in the frenzied metabolism of the mind.

And yet, despite how reasonable this explanation sounds, how unassailably sensible, she knows without a doubt that she is not dreaming. She is wide awake.

"Come suck, come suck, come suck," the voice says now, the words clipped and sharp and suddenly clear, insistent, spoken as the veiled head wheels around to stare at her, *into* her, but instead of the face she expects to see—the face of a woman, a mother—she finds herself staring into a recess of complete and utter darkness, a total absence of light, save for two half-moons of white bone, accenting deep cavities where the eyes should be.

"Come," it commands, and now that the body is angled toward her, desiccated, cadaverous, naked beneath the shroud, she can see what is being cradled, what is being fed and nurtured and kept close.

A serpent: hulking and albinotic with ravenous red eyes, lap-cradled and coiled tight except for head and tail—the tail flicking idly, teasingly against the shroud, rippling the shadowy fabric; the spade-shaped head lifted up and back, fangs buried in the offered breast, frothing milk and blood; the muscles in the serpent's neck undulating, drawing deep.

Twenty-One

Simone is going to Mass for the third time in her life, and all three times at the same little church—what is it called again? She can never remember.

She'd waited as long as she could to call Adam, waited until she could see the first streaks of dawn against the clouds, sometime after six. She waited in terror, unable to sleep after what she'd seen. Adam answered quickly, already on his way to the nursing home for the morning shift. In rapid, halting half sentences, she tried to tell him what happened, what she saw, and every word that tumbled out of her mouth filled her with frustration and shame. She knew how crazy she sounded.

"Are you sure you weren't dreaming?" Of course he asked this, the only possible response that a reasonable person could have, parroting the same question she'd asked herself dozens of times.

But then he said something she didn't expect. "Maybe it's Mary."

"*Mary?*" she repeated, incredulously.

"Yeah, there's this famous image of Mary with a snake. It's from the Bible, I think. I don't know the details—that's more my mom's thing."

"But Adam, this was ..." She trailed off. To her, the Virgin Mary was a saccharine, pastel projection of idealized femininity, docile and facile and sweet. Whatever she'd seen last night, it was not *sweet*. It didn't even have a *face*. But, then again, what did she know? There was a darker side to Catholicism, the bleeding statues, the corpses under the altars. Maybe Mary had a dark side too.

"Look, I gotta go." Adam's voice was thin and crackly through the phone. "But you should talk to the priest in town. Mom likes him, and she's hard to please. Especially when it comes to priests."

So here she is, nothing better to do with her frantic, cold-sweat energy than follow Adam's advice. Anything to get out of the house, to have a momentary quest.

Mass has already begun by the time she enters the church. She can hear the drone of voices murmuring in unison as she pauses in the foyer, tapping snow from her boots, second-guessing herself. She lingers momentarily by the small side table, the rack of plastic rosaries, the doe-eyed, pink-cheeked placard saints. *How can anyone believe in this stuff?* she wonders, reaching out to touch one of the beveled rosary beads. Take One, says the handwritten sign, and then she remembers—she already did.

She digs her hands into her coat pockets, searching; the pockets are deep, almost down to her knees, but there at the bottom of one she finds it, fingers feeling for the glasslike beads but finding instead the right-angled edges of the crucifix as they dig into her palm—plastic but still somehow sharp. She draws back her hand.

The voices are singing together now, off-key and acapella, and she uses the sound as cover to sneak in through the back, sitting in the last pew again, but on the right-hand side this time, able to survey the space from a different angle. She confirms quickly, with great relief, that Helen is not among the gathered few.

A man has begun to read at the lectern, a voice she recognizes—Miguel. He's saying something stern and Old Testament sounding, something about God sending a messenger the people apparently want but who also seems terrifying.

"Who will endure the day of his coming?" Miguel is asking, then something about a fire and sacrifice—or maybe the messenger *is* the fire? Turning hearts of fathers toward children, children toward fathers ... Is this a promise or a warning? A threat? It's hard to tell, since Miguel is reading in a flat, quiet monotone. "Lest I come and strike the land with doom." He stops and lets the word hang in the air for a bit and then everyone's murmuring, "Thanks be to God."

Then there's someone else reading and everyone repeating back this one line—how do they know what to say and when to say it? "Lift up your heads and see," they are saying, "your redemption is near at hand." They keep repeating it in this robotic, flattened way, three, four times now, each time the words piling on Simone like invisible weights, stones with hooks that hang from her shoulders, her arms, her head, until what they are demanding feels impossible. How can she lift up her head and see, when there is this heaviness pulling her toward the ground? Is this what redemption is supposed to feel like? Being crushed?

And all at once, as if they've rushed upon her, she is aware of the images encircling the room, over a dozen similar images lined up all along the sides of the sanctuary, one hanging just two feet above her—all scenes of suffering and longing; nothing concealed there, no private pain, just open, gaping anguish.

Looming next to her, over her, three feet tall, is a wooden carving of a woman holding a man's lifeless body. The woman clutches him, presses him against her chest, straining with the burden of the corpse that is already half laid in the grave, as if pulled by its own dead weight. Her face is sick with grief, her body held against his as if she wants to be a corpse herself, to descend into the grave with him—but the pain on her face is a signal of life; she is not dead, but in agony. A silent agony that no words can reach.

Simone looks away, first up toward the priest, who is now walking over to the pulpit with a red book, then quickly back down because she doesn't want to see the dying, bleeding body hanging over them, that same body encircling them in dramatic displays of torment and death. All the bodies in the sanctuary—so many of them!—somehow move without moving, speak without speaking. She tries in vain to decipher the story they are trying to tell.

Maybe her mother was right. Maybe this is just some masochistic cult: death-obsessed, life-denying, woman-hating. Is this why she feels so unsettled, conflicted? Pulled toward, yet afraid to look? Repulsed, yet drawn?

She thinks of the other American churches she's occasionally meandered through, most of them displaying a clean, abstract beauty, gesturing toward *something*, but vaguely. There might be a framed image of Jesus somewhere, softly glowing, gentle. There might be a cross, but emptied of body and blood. There would be few bodies at all, and certainly no *female* ones. No women saints, no mother of God.

She tries to probe her heart, plucking strings, searching for the source of her discomfort. There is something off-putting here, but not for the reasons her mother claimed. Almost the opposite. No erasure of women or absence of eros—instead, an excess, an extremity, a flagrant display of desire and reckless vulnerability. The chest opened and the heart exposed. In the carved, thrown-back faces and parted lips, she glimpses her own obscure depths, the buried root of her own aimless desire, the source of the ache. She glimpses this like one approaching the edge of an abyss—and pulls back.

Everyone is standing now, and she rises to join them numbly, her body moving of its own accord. The priest begins to read, but her attention is elsewhere; her eyes rove the room looking for some sign, some interpretive key that will make it all make sense, that will somehow explain why she is here, right now, in a room full of arcane symbols that are speaking in a strange, wordless language that she doesn't understand.

It is then that she notices a warm, diffuse light coming from the opposite side of the sanctuary. The light wavers and fluctuates, tremulating like water. There's a hidden chamber there, she realizes, a cave-like alcove that must be lit from within by candlelight. From where she is, she can't see inside. She can tell only that there is an opening.

"What, then, will this child be?"

The words reach her, clear as a struck bell. The priest has said them—she saw his lips form the words—but the sound comes from somewhere behind and above her, as if not spoken by a man at all, but a woman.

Simone looks sharply behind her but sees no one, and, glancing around, she sees that no other heads have turned. They are all still looking toward the priest and mumbling something in unison, now sitting down all together, a herd of docile sheep.

She tries to catch the priest after Mass, but he disappears through a little door at the back of the sanctuary. The space has emptied quickly, no one so much as glancing at her as they file out, hastily dipping their fingers in a bowl of water by the door, heads burrowed in the collars of their coats.

Unsure what to do with herself, she pretends to contemplate the carvings along the church wall, the scenes of the crucifixion, walking slowly with her head cocked to the side as if perusing an art gallery.

Abruptly, without warning, between the fourth and fifth carvings, the wall separates, as if an entirely new passageway has sprung into being, some secret chamber. The opening is long and narrow, tunnel-like, containing within the source of the flickering light she'd seen earlier and quickly forgotten.

Her pulse begins to race; she glances quickly around as if expecting someone to stop her, to tell her harshly that she is trespassing. But no one is there. No one, and yet—she can't shake the sensation that she is being watched.

She ducks into the alcove quickly, feeling the impulse to hide—which vanishes as soon as she's inside, as if she's walked through an invisible curtain into another world. At the back of the chamber, the end of the arched tunnel, is a large icon, so large it takes up the entire wall, leaving room only for a small kneeler and a rack of bottled white candles, a third of which are lit. The icon is unlike any she's ever seen—not a solo portrait of some aloof, sad-eyed saint, but an image of an entire cosmos, an icon full of icons.

Stretched across the icon's center are two overlapping squares with curved sides, like tents thrown open, the squares offset so that the eight points form a star. This two-layered star is hung upon a mat of three concentric circles—red, orange, and yellow like the sun—the star itself a layering of red upon purple. Anchoring this purple layer, one in each corner, are four creatures, mythical-looking hybrids, one of them a winged ox, maybe, and something like a griffin or a lion.

At the center of the layered star, set against the edges of the red tent, is a series of more circles, and circles within circles—an outer circle the color of the sea, but filled with strange six-winged creatures with human faces, all gathered around an inner circle, darker blue, which holds the figure of a woman, shown from the waist up, her arms held up and open.

The woman appears to be looming up out of the dark blue circle, her halo like the rising moon, and on her breast, nested within another three-layered globe, is a child, robed in gold, his halo set against a deep blue ring of stars. He has one hand raised in blessing; the other holds a cup.

They seem to be signaling to her, the woman and the child, their large, dark eyes looking through her, past her, fixed upon something that she cannot see.

Are the circles spinning? Ever so slightly, but somehow in motion? Or just the candlelight, perhaps, giving the illusion of some inner, animating force.

The *click* of a lock behind her, echoing in the empty space; the sound of an opening door. She hurries out of the alcove, backing away, eyes still drawn to the image but retreating hastily, instinctively.

The priest has reemerged, no longer clad in the long, shimmering robes but standard clerical garb: black shirt and pants with a small white square at his throat. "Oh!" He is surprised to see her standing there, sprung seemingly from nowhere. He had been moving quickly, as if he had somewhere else to be.

"Hi, um, Father"—the word is awkward and heavy on her lips—"you don't know me, but my name is Simone, and I'm an old friend of the Hoffmanns." She blushes at the fib, knowing Helen would not think of her as anything close to a friend, but at the sound of the name, the priest nods, so she continues. He seems distracted as she begins, attempting a veneer of placidity, but his eyes keep darting around the room, as if looking for an exit.

She starts with the first appearance, the veiled figure at the foot of the bed, keeping her description concise and unembellished, watching the priest's face carefully for signs of approval, but he seems unfazed. Maybe it's a common thing for Catholics to wake up and see a veiled woman by their bed. "And the second time, the next night, there was a snake."

The priest perks up a little at this. "Ah, a snake, yes, under her feet?"

She hesitates.

"She's crushing it, yes?"

"Not exactly."

"What, then?" The priest is staring at her through his round spectacles. She finally has his attention.

"She's ..." Simone cradles her arms awkwardly, moving them back and forth, as if rocking an invisible infant, not wanting to say aloud what she saw, not wanting to say the word *breast* in front of a priest.

"She was ... feeding it. Holding it and feeding it...." She gestures toward her chest. "From here."

"*Dios mío*," he whispers under his breath, swiftly crossing himself.

"I came to you because ... someone told me it might be Mary?"

The priest stares at her, unblinking. "That's not Mary."

After a leaden silence, during which she tries to grasp the implications of his words, the priest starts speaking again, vigorously this time, his gestures emphatic.

She must go to confession, he says, as soon as possible, right now.

"No, no, I'm not Catholic, I'm just ..."

The house needs to be blessed, he says, as soon as possible—but not right now. "It's a busy time." He glances apologetically toward a large wreath near the altar with pink and purple candles, all lit, and Simone remembers that it is December 23, the day before Christmas Eve.

He can come the day after Christmas, he says, three days from now, but Simone demurs. No, no, she's only staying there temporarily; it's not her house, she might be gone by then.

At this he disappears through the narrow door, re-emerging with something in his hands, a plastic vial of water and a glass vial of coarse white grains. "Holy water and exorcised salt," he says. "Very powerful. But," he adds, peering over his spectacles at her, "not as powerful as confession."

She takes the water and salt reluctantly but without protest, feeling it would be rude to decline, having imposed upon his time, something she already regrets. She's not sure what she expected, going to a priest. Perhaps she'd hoped for some kind of reassurance that there was nothing to worry about, that this was a good omen somehow or just psychological projection—a potent metaphor perhaps, but nothing to fear. Most of the clergy she's crossed paths with have been big into metaphors, heaven and hell as internal states and all that.

But this priest is not reassuring. He is communicating urgency. There is an unnerving sternness in his manner now, a paternal severity, like a doctor urging his patient to let him treat a festering wound.

She murmurs her thanks and turns away, letting the water and salt fall into the deep recesses of her pocket, clinking softly against the plastic rosary. She feels lopsided now, one side of her heavy with superstition, the other side hanging empty.

The priest calls out to her, as if one last thought has just occurred to him. "They don't just attach to houses ..." But she's already exiting the sanctuary, the doors closing softly behind her, his words just reaching her through the narrowing gap. She pretends not to hear.

Miguel is waiting for her outside the church. He's pulling a cigarette from a pack and offers her one. "I heard you talking to Father. I shouldn't have been listening, but"—he shrugs, hunching to light his cigarette, hands cupped around the flame—"I know who you saw."

"You do?"

"Yeah. I've seen it before. But never here, in the States. It's weird. I've never heard about it attached to a gringa before. No offense."

"I mean, I wouldn't say it's *attached*, not to *me* anyway." Simone can feel her frustration rising. These Catholics are acting as if she has some incurable affliction, as if she's tainted somehow. "Maybe the house is haunted, I don't know. I don't really believe in ghosts. I don't really believe in any of this. Maybe I'm imagining or hallucinating it all."

He shakes his head. "No, it's real." He says this matter-of-factly, casually, as if talking about the weather or baseball scores.

"Well, what is it?"

"Santa Muerte."

"Muerte—isn't that—"

"Death, yeah. Nuestra Señora de la Santa Muerte."

"Our Lady of . . ."

"Our Lady of Holy Death."

"So it *is* like a Catholic thing? Like one of those Marian visions?" Simone can feel her credulity straining, a thin, taut thread about to snap.

"No, no. It's not Mary. Father's right about that. It's not human."

Simone hesitates, momentarily distracted by the implied notion of the Virgin Mary as human—not an archetype or a symbol, but an actual person.

"Is it dangerous? Santa Muerte? I mean, what does it want?"

"Depends who you ask. My aunt had a shrine to La Flaca, and she swore it helped her get all kinds of things. Money, a better house, protection." He shrugs again, taking a drag from the cigarette. "She does have a really nice house."

"So . . . maybe it *is* a good"—Simone isn't sure what word to use—"spirit?" She thinks of her conversation with

Cass, remembers the medium's words, tries to gather herself around them for comfort, as if warming her hands over a fire. "I mean, what do you think?"

"Me?" Miguel exhales out the side of his mouth, flicking his half-spent cigarette onto the icy sidewalk, grinding it under his heel. "I think it's the devil."

Twenty-Two

She has decided not to call him. Or at least—to test the decision, to try it on, for at least a few hours. Her hand itches for the phone, itches to feel it come to life in her palm, to see it wake up, all full of light and color and possibility, waiting to take her wherever she wished. But she fights the urge, lets the phone sit alone on the counter, a mournful black slab.

They've had no communication since her frenetic call to him this morning. She knows he was working all day, that he would probably be off by now. Waiting, maybe. Or resisting, like she was.

She knows also that he is married, and he knows that she knows, even though they never talked about it, only talked around it, around *her*, in wide circles. But there have been little clues, hints of upheaval, of recurrent separations, repeated moves back to the family farm, then back into town. He spoke as if it were just *him*—"I was staying on the farm for a bit then"—but she knows. She saw the ring.

They'd walked right up to the threshold yesterday, out on the snow, approaching the point of transgression, but they didn't cross it. They flirted with crossing, lingered at the open door. She'd thought then that it was only a matter of time, that they were standing on a path that was moving forward of its own accord, like a conveyer belt, but now, for some strange reason, she wants to see if she can step off the path, pivot in a different direction. She feels like testing the strength of her will, as if flexing and stretching an underused muscle.

Without the active distraction of Adam—it is now a *passive* distraction, like a cat coiled up in the corner of the room, ignored but still watching—she is left to face her own thoughts, her own jumbled-up memories that ping her out of nowhere, in no chronological order. The house is teeming with them, little rodents darting out of the dark, then scurrying back as soon as approached.

It's strange—the memories are clearer the further back she goes. The childhood memories surface easily in her mind, vibrant images, whole scenes, like a home movie she can play on demand. But in adolescence, instead of following a neat, straight line, the past begins to spiral, loop back on itself, slowly at first, but then rapidly like a cyclone; the last few months she spent in this house are a whirling blur.

When she tries to make sense of that time, her senior year, she can remember a basic summary, some key plot points; she could describe in broad strokes what happened. But the content of the memories, the emotional depth and links of causality—it is as if a veil has been thrown over them. She knows, for example, that she and Adam broke up; she knows this happened in heated whispers in the food court of the mall in Idaho Falls; she remembers a woman at the next table over looking at her pityingly. But the *why*, the content of those sharp words, and more than that, the state of her heart in that moment—had she wanted to leave or was she fighting to stay?—was rolled up and tucked away, just out of reach. It is as if that time, the months before she left town for good, was not something she experienced directly, but rather a story that had been told to her, and when she tries to go back there, she runs into the synopsis, the official report, rather than the event itself.

She's stretched out on the couch, wrapped up in her blue coat, using it almost like a sleeping bag, shifting and burrowing into the cushions, trying to get comfortable. Something's jabbing into her side—that damn crucifix. She sits up, digs around in her pocket, remembering just as her fingers touch them: the water and the salt. She pulls them out, all tangled in the string of beads, which she shakes off and tosses on the coffee table. She stares at the vials, one in each hand. Such ordinary substances, the most ordinary, save perhaps for the dust of the earth. How could something so ordinary possibly carry any power? She is struck with the impulse to taste them, to gobble them up, to rinse the water and salt down her throat. What would happen then? Would demons fly out of her belly? She smirks. "Well, what the hell," she says aloud. She has nothing better to do. Maybe this will occupy her hands, which are still itching for the phone, for Adam.

As soon as she stands, ready to proceed, she realizes she has no idea what to do. Does she just sprinkle a few grains and drops in each room? Or should she make some kind of circle on the ground? No, that doesn't sound right. That's more of a witchy thing. And then she will be stuck inside the circle for protection. Better to keep it simple.

She begins in her mother's room, planning to move clockwise and up, ending in her old bedroom. She tries to recall *The Exorcist*, some prayer or incantation, but all that comes to mind is a line from *Macbeth*.

"Out, damned spot," she says boldly, theatrically. "Begone!" Gently tapping the vial, she makes a small pile of salt in her palm, then flings it toward the corners of the room, hearing a faint rustle as the grains fall. The holy water has a spout that pops up. She flicks her wrist and a line of droplets falls across the floor in an arc. "Begone!" she says again.

Over and over, in each room gaining a sense of confidence, she scatters the salt and the water, ushering out whatever might be lurking in the shadows. She proceeds with a spirit of boldness and levity, both devil-may-care and bemused.

Yet when she approaches the door to her bedroom, a door that sits slightly ajar, a door that is open but still requires her hand to push through into the waiting dark, her levity evaporates all at once, effervescent little bubbles popping into nothing, and is replaced by the sensation of dread, cold and brick-like, in the pit of her belly.

She has little salt left; the water is all but gone. Why hadn't she started *here*? The epicenter of whatever was happening? So obvious now, but the thought hadn't occurred to her when she began, perhaps because it had all seemed like a joke, a game—until she'd walked through the barely open door. This keeps happening: In the light of day, away from this room, her fear gives way easily to skepticism, to the default assumption that whatever is happening, the source has to be inside her head. But when she is *here*, the presence of whatever inhabits the house feels as real as the presence of a person or an animal—something alive.

"Begone," she says, only managing a whisper, shaking the last grains of salt in a jagged line across the floor. She flicks the water, a diffident gesture, furtive. The last drops dribble out onto her hand and run down her wrist, absorbed quickly by the ribbed cuff of her coat.

She's near the light switch now, but instead of flicking it on, she begins to retreat, backing away slowly, closing the door firmly once safely outside.

"Son of a bitch," she says, in a long exhale. "Holy hell." She will sleep on the couch tonight.

On her way back to the living room, she takes a quick detour—the empty vials go in the kitchen trash, her phone back in her hand. She'll keep it nearby, just in case.

Twenty-Three

She walks through the front door and sees her mother sitting at the table, back turned. Mother is wearing her white coat from the clinic, hands moving busily. She can hear Mother's lips murmur. Mother is counting. She ventures closer, around to the side, sees what Mother is counting: pills. Tiny towers of pills, arranged in front of Mother in a neat row, pills of all shapes and pastel hues.

"This is for your depression," says Mother, pushing a tower of oblong whites toward her. "Anxiety," a wobbling stack of pink. "Birth control, you can never be too careful," a wheel of discs standing upright, encased in plastic and foil, gradations of blue.

"And this"—Mother turns, hand open and outstretched, as if she's holding something living in her hand, a reptile that might skuttle away—"this is the way out."

She looks at the offered hand, the neat row of tiny hexagons, so miniscule and sterile and safe, and something begins to writhe deep within her, something muted and angry, awake now and clawing its way out, up into her throat, where it lodges, trapped. She opens her mouth and tries to scream, scream it out, *get it out*, but there is nothing, nothing, not even air, just her gaping, distended mouth, her contracting throat, laboring to release a cry that won't come.

Twenty-Four

She's awakened by an agonized moan, like someone trying to scream through a mouthful of water—who is it, so close to her? Who is screaming?

Me, she realizes, *it is me*. She is screaming, a strangled scream struggling up from a still-paralyzed throat, closed mouth, her mind awake but her body still trapped in sleep.

Wake up, she urges herself, struggling to move her limbs, which are prone like the dead. *Wake. Up.*

Her eyes are partially open, little slits fixed on the double French doors that mark off the entrance to the living room. She closed the doors last night, testing the knob satisfactorily before letting herself fall asleep.

But now, she is watching them separate, drift apart slowly, the hinges protesting with a protracted creak. Opening. Making way.

Something is coming down the stairs. Even through her half-closed eyes she can see the dark shape moving steadily down, down, too substantial for a shadow, seeming to float just above each stair yet somehow making the distinct sound of footfall. Her ears—wide awake and attuned, on alert—can hear the wood groan with each step.

She begins to panic. Her senses are awake, feeding her this data, warning her, urging her, and yet she remains paralyzed, able to watch and listen, but unable to move, to run while there is still time, maybe, to rush out of the room and out the front door before the thing descends, before it turns along the curved stairs and onto the main floor. But this route would require rushing *toward* it, gambling that its pace would remain unchanged, that it would not flash suddenly in front of her and wrap her in its dark veil, thin and rubbery like the wings of a bat.

Or she could run *away*, fling open a window and rip out the screen, dive into the snow, drive off—but wait, where are her car keys?

Hanging by the front door.

The various scenarios race through her roving, raving mind quick-fire, one after another, in the space between each plodding step, all theoretical because her limbs lie numbed, as if under thrall, unresponsive. How can her body defy her control like this? How can it mutiny?

It's rounding the corner now, it's turning, facing her. She can see the white crescents of the cheekbones, the lipless teeth stretched and grinning, a death grin; it is all shadow except for these and one exposed forearm, one skeletal claw outstretched and holding a small globe that churns with pale light, staring at her like a fitful, clouded eye.

Another option occurs—call for help. She can see her phone on the coffee table next to her, just inches from her hand; her mind spins through the people she could call—Cass, maybe, or Miguel; they would believe her, she needs someone who would believe her; maybe even Peter, so far away, yet his voice might reassure her somehow, might be a thread she could follow to find her way out of this maze, this labyrinthine house that has entrapped her, not just here and now but for *years*, ever since—

Adam.

She does not think his name but hears it, her vigilant ears grasping it from the air, a long-tailed whisper. She echoes it, exhaling the name on her breath, and as it passes her lips, her body relaxes, her limbs spring into motion as if a spell has been lifted, a trap suddenly sprung, her hand is grasping the phone, fingers stroking madly, searching for his name, then hearing his voice, hearing herself say, "Adam, please, something is happening; you have to come here, now."

Twenty-Five

The sun coaxes her awake—first her mind, an awareness of daylight, of place, but not yet of time—the world glowing red orange beyond her eyelids, still closed. For a stretched-out moment, on the liminal edge of half sleep, she thinks she is sixteen again; she thinks she is back in the warm haze of that first *morning after*, her mind dizzy with the realization that she is no longer a virgin, that she's tasted the enticing fruit and become wise, privy now to a secret knowledge; she's become someone new. *I have to tell Cass*, she thinks, before remembering, like a fuzzy picture slowly coming to focus, that Cass is no longer her best friend, that that first morning happened over sixteen years ago, long ago, back at the halfway mark of her current lifespan.

Somehow, she's looped back; this current moment, this *morning after*, is an echo, a spontaneous restaging of that first free fall.

She keeps her eyes closed as her mind slowly surfaces, reorienting to the present, piecing together the jumbled, churning images of the night before. The paralysis, the thing coming down the stairs, her panicked call to Adam—how it all stopped as soon as she made that call, everything but her fear, which kept her cowering, curled up in a fetal ball on the couch until she heard Adam's voice calling outside, his brief knock before pushing open the door, his heavy boots crossing the now-deserted front room. Then he was next to her, his arms around her, and terror gave way to desire.

How quickly and wordlessly it had unfolded from there, how easily they fell into a once-familiar dance, eventually making their way into her old room. Who was leading? Who was following? It was hard to tell. They stumbled up the stairs together.

And now here they are, entangled.

Maybe that had been the plan all along—but whose plan? Some capricious spirit? Or a manifestation of her own psyche? Does it make a difference? Whatever it was, this force had pulled them back together, and in the honeyed glow of the late-morning sun, that is all that seems to matter.

She lets herself sink into it, that feeling—that warm, languid feeling, like she is drunk on sweet nectar, swimming in it. That feeling lingers, suffusing the house, suffusing them both; she can see it pooling in his eyes, liquid and golden, twin mirrors. They wallow in it all morning, first in bed, half dozing, then ambling around the kitchen together, exchanging looks but few words, glancing at each other, then away, as if speaking will disrupt the dreamlike haze.

And then, after coffee and toast, with a goodbye kiss, as if they are some long-married couple and this is an ordinary morning, Adam is gone—off to work, he says. She watches him leave, standing in the open doorway, an afghan draped around her shoulders even though the cold doesn't seem to touch her.

When she steps back into the house—the house that all morning has been approvingly, indulgently quiet, like a parent gazing down at a sleeping child—and closes the front door, the *click* of the lock sliding into place is like a switch that flips, and immediately the atmosphere of the room is altered. The drowsy warmth dries up like a pool rapidly evaporating, sucked dry, and in its place is a buzzing, whirring energy, so potent she swears she can hear it. She even pauses by the light switch, bending her ear toward it, wondering whether something is wrong with the wiring. But the energy isn't in the walls; it isn't electric, it's atmospheric—it's in the air, the churning air.

We must be together. We must be together. It's as if the house itself is speaking, urging her, prodding her. *We must be together.*

She whispers the words aloud. "We must be together." Yes, this is it, the path, the fate that she's been flailing around for; this is the reason she came back *here*—she's been *drawn* back, everything is converging. She is meant for that first love, and he is meant for her. She can feel her heartbeat quickening, matching the steam-engine cadence of the urgent house-whisper. *We must be together.*

There's only one thing in the way. That bud, that bloom inside her body. Everything else can be easily shorn; she can quit her job, break up with Peter—there is a pang at this, a thin spear in the heart, but she hardens herself against it. Adam is her fate; this is *meant*. All her belongings are easy enough to move or replace; she can scrap her life and return here, fully, to be reconciled with the past, with Adam, with everything she left behind.

But first, she must do what she came here to do.

She's climbing the stairs now, only vaguely aware of having decided to ascend them; she is not moving herself as much as being moved.

And look, there! What is that? That shimmering, shining, flickering shape hovering over the top step? She slows her pace reverently, filled with awe, her eyes fixed, hungrily feasting on the most beautiful thing she's ever seen.

A column of color and light rising upward, wavering, gathering itself into a form that remains visible yet unstable, the contours shifting like a white flame, but a flame that curves outward at the top, almost bulblike—less like a flame, perhaps, than a tornado of light and air. And all down the funnel, which as she stares seems more and more like a body, a long torso, is a vertical row of dazzling jewels, jewels like eyes, glinting and catching the light, casting rainbow fragments around the room. She glances down at herself, gasping in delight, to see strips of colored light dancing across her belly, her arms and hands, adorning her.

In this array of dazzling light the dread she has been feeling—feeling, yes, but suppressing, thinking-not-thinking about the tiny white hexagons that will dissolve inside her, convulse her womb, the blood that will follow—vanishes entirely, as if sucked up by the jewel eyes and shattered into color shards against the wall, gone. No dread now, but euphoria, a heady, bubbly joy coursing through her, filling her with energy, her body and mind pulsing, in tandem with the house. *We must be together, we must be together.*

She steps closer just as the vision moves backward—or is the vision pulling her forward? She can see now how the funnel seems to bend near the floor, stretching behind the column of eyes, tail-like. She steps forward as it slides backward, the bulbous end—is it a head?—swaying from side to side like a pendulum.

In the center of this head, if it is a head, is the largest of the jewels, a diamond-shaped abyss of light, an orifice of mirrors, each capturing a reflected fragment of her own face.

The scintillating vision leads her to the door of the bedroom and vanishes. Just like that, in a blink, she's staring at the blank face of the door, which is cracked open. All she has to do is step forward and push. All she has to do is walk across the room and open her suitcase, dig around for the white paper bag, and shake its contents free. All she has to do is listen to the urging of the house, to follow its lead. And she does.

Twenty-Six

She's driving into town with a scrap of paper on her lap, a hastily scrawled shopping list: pads, ibuprofen, hot water bottle, tea, chocolate.

This is perfect, she's telling herself, it's Christmas Eve; Adam will no doubt be seeing family over the holiday. She will tell him she is under the weather and hunker down for two days, and when she sees him again, if she's still bleeding, she'll just say she's on her period—he will never know! No one will ever know.

"No one will know. No one will know." She hears herself chanting the words under her breath, in the same repetitive rhythm as the whispers in the house, which seem to be following her, even as she speeds along in the opposite direction. Speeding, yes, but why is she in such a rush? She pulses the brake, tries to calm herself, but that *energy*, that frenetic, pulsing energy that entered her back at the house cannot be quelled. It carries her along like a current.

The empty chants run on a loop in her brain—*no one will know, we must be together*—automatic, unconscious, her mind elsewhere, transfixed by the memory of the dazzling vision that had led her up the stairs. It had to be a sign, an omen, a message from the universe that the choice she is making is the right one, the one that will set her free—free to find her love, her fate. How could it be false? It had chased away the evil omen, the thing Miguel had called the devil. There was good and evil after all; fear was evil, and light and love were on the side of good.

This town, she thinks this as she breaches its borders, passing by the welcome sign, has upended everything, everything she thought she knew. She would be a new person here, reinvent herself. Maybe, as Adam's wife—surely they would get married, once he was free—she could live simply and close to the earth and learn to make things like yogurt and sourdough and soap.

"Scented soap," she whispers under her breath, catching a flash in her periphery of angled color and light. Is it the vision? Has it followed her here? But when she looks to the side, nothing.

She's passing the nursing home—Adam, he's in there!—and on a whim she wheels hard to the right. She will pop in, surprise him. She imagines stealing a kiss in the corner of an empty hallway or behind a closed door. If anyone sees her, she will pretend she doesn't know him, that she's come to visit someone else. Adam will understand; he will read her silent signals.

She parks and giddily jogs to the door, so full of inner fire that she doesn't bother to put on her coat, which she's flung into the back seat like sloughed-off skin.

Impervious. The word bubbles up. "Impervious," she whispers.

The doors whisk open, sensing her presence, and as they do, she sees a flash of red—angry, glaring red, the red of a fierce, flashing jeweled eye that stops her cold.

It is a warning, she realizes, something doesn't want her here, and she hesitates before the second set of automatic doors, wondering whether she should turn around, retreat. Is this the evil omen or the good one?

But the thought of someone, something, trying to keep her from Adam propels her forward; she *has* to see him now, to make sure that last night meant what she thought it meant. One look in his eyes and she'll know.

She hoped to see him as soon as she walked down the hall; the place is so small, how hard would he be to find? But there is no one around, no sound except the tinny baritone of Bing Crosby echoing from the common room. She follows the sound, glancing into rooms as she goes. No one. The common room is deserted too, perhaps newly so, a half-emptied puzzle box open on the table, a vacant recliner askew and bobbing slightly. Where are all the people?

"Can I help you." Not a question but an accusation. She turns sharply; there's a nurse behind her, arms folded, blue eyes boring into her like ice picks. Simone is too startled to lie.

"I'm looking for Adam. Is Adam here?"

The nurse's mouth curls into a smirk, as if she expected this question, as if she's heard it before.

"Not here. He's off until the twenty-seventh, lucky bastard." The nurse waits, still staring, almost hungrily awaiting Simone's reaction.

"Oh." Simone edges backward. "Oh yes, that's right. I do remember him saying ... Yes. The twenty-seventh. Thank you."

The nurse is not yet finished with her; this will be her day's highlight, this turn of the screw. "Do you want to leave a message for him?"

"No, no. I can text him. I have his number."

"Oh, I'm sure you do."

It is clear now that the nurse is not going to kindly accept surrender, so clearly signaled by Simone's weak and nervous smile, her breathless, hand-waving responses, her attempt at retreat. She stands fixed in Simone's path, a sneering brick wall; Simone is forced to skirt around her, head down, hurrying away from her parting words. "Have yourself a merry Christmas, now."

Simone scurries around the corner blindly, colliding with a skeletal figure curled up in a wheelchair, her legs striking against a sharp, bent-up knee.

Alice. Gleeful, contorted, gasping with laughter, her clouded eyes taunting, her mouth agape in mocking delight, interrupting Simone's stream of reflexive, hollow apologies with a rasping cry. "You let it in, you let it in!" She claws at Simone's arm, pulling her close, down into the rot of her breath. "Now you're like me."

Simone pulls away, stumbling back, and hastens toward the doors, running as if being chased, but the only thing following her is the sound of Alice's hollow laughter, all twisted up in the cheery singsong lilt of the music echoing through the halls.

To face unafraid, the plans that we've made, walking in a winter wonderland . . .

Twenty-Seven

She would have been fine with just a basket, but she's chosen a cart anyway, a cart with a bent front wheel that protests and pulls hard to the left; her arm muscles are taut with the effort to keep it straight. Pushing the cart in circles, aimlessly, meandering through the half-dozen aisles of the grocery store, her eyes passing over the neat rows of objects but registering none of them, her attention caught up entirely in the eddy of one revolving thought.

He lied.

Adam had lied. "Gotta get to work," he'd said, one of the few things either of them had said that morning. But that's not where he went, and he had not wanted her to know where he would be. If she hadn't stopped, impulsively, at the nursing home, she wouldn't know. Whatever had wanted to stop her from going there had wanted to hide the lie.

The obvious explanation is that he's with another woman, maybe the woman who was (is?) his wife, or maybe, even worse, another girlfriend. She doesn't really know him, after all—the thought sneaks through even as she deflects it; no, she *does* know him, better than anyone, because she knew him first. But is the boy she knew then—sincere, innocent, naïve to the ways of love—the man he is now?

A contest, it seems, is emerging in her mind, her heart. A debate. Some Socratic impulse to test what she longs to be true. *Do I really know him? What does it mean to know someone?*

She stops the cart in front of the hygiene section, scanning the bright plastic wrapping for what she might need. There are so many options, even in this little store, so many possible combinations of thinness, length, absorbency, pads for daytime, pads for overnight, pads for light days, pads for heavy days, pads with wings. How heavy is a miscarriage? And is it heavier when forced? She tries to remember. How many days would she bleed? The instructions had been vague: a few days to a few weeks. Weeks!

She's drawn to a fuchsia-colored package emblazoned with the image of an athletic woman leaping over a hurdle, her body bent forward, flexed with speed and power. But those pads are flimsy, meant for only occasional drips. With a sigh, she grabs a bulky package with generic branding, no images at all, not even a single flower petal, and tosses it into the cart.

Despite this unwanted revelation—well, half of a revelation, really; a lie has been revealed, but not yet the truth—she is proceeding as planned, gathering the necessary supplies, staying the course. But the energy that had carried her there has dwindled, ebbing to a low-grade, anxious hum. The urgent whispers are gone.

This is better, she assures herself. *Now I'm doing this for me, not for a man.*

For the first time since arriving in Fall River, she feels an urge to call Cynthia, to hear once more what she's always been told, what every doctor has told her, including the one who prescribed her these pills. *Safe. Effective.* She knows so well what Cynthia would say that she rehearses the talking points in her head. She's worked so hard to get where she is. She almost has tenure; she's almost succeeded in a system built for men, where the years of peak pressure, peak achievement, overlap with a woman's childbearing years. "You have to game the system," Cynthia would say, has already said. "Just like I had to do."

Only an hour ago, she'd been fantasizing about walking away from it all, about making her own damn *soap*, not gaming the system but leaving it altogether. If she was doing this for *herself*, which one was her real self? The self she'd been all her adult life, molded in the shape of her mother, or the self that she abandoned at age sixteen? (But who is this "she" doing the abandoning? Who is the "she" who is choosing?)

Unbidden, Peter comes to mind, despite her continued attempts to lock him out. "Come back down to earth," he'd say to her when she got like this, all caught up in her anxious thoughts. Peter is like earth, solid and grounded. She is more like air, easily tossed about, and also like water, changeable. And Adam? To her, he is a fire, consuming. The spark is still there, underneath the uncertainty, the apparent betrayal, not snuffed out but smoldering.

She's heading for her last stop, the candy section. What kind of chocolate will bring her solace when she's bleeding alone in the dark?

Maybe it's the sickly blend of all the different kinds of sweetness—fruit chews, chocolate, licorice, bubble gum—just after walking past the air fresheners—lavender, pine, citrus, vanilla—but as she stands and looks at the shiny rows of candy bars, a wave of nausea ripples up from under her ribs right into her throat, so forcefully she claps a hand across her mouth, using the other to steady herself against the metal shelving, holding perfectly still, sure she is about to spew half-digested coffee and toast all over the polished concrete floor.

Why are the smells so intense here? The coffee, the slabs of raw meat, the fried food simmering under heat lamps, the chemical odor of the plastic toys and balloons—everything is rank, as if smell could be cranked up like sound.

And then she realizes why. This is a sign of heightened vigilance, her body's newfound sensitivity to possible dangers, things not safe to eat, things that could pose a danger, not to her, but to what is inside her. Her body is *aware*; it *knows* and is already working to shelter the fragile, precarious life unfurling within her. And here she is planning to thwart that protection, disarm it, trick her body into relinquishing what it instinctively wants to protect.

I've boarded the train and there's no getting off.

The train is her body, humming along, doing what it is designed to do.

The wave of nausea dissipates, and she stands up straight, regains her composure; breathing deeply, she exits the aisle. Chocolate, it seems, will bring no comfort, only revulsion. The only thing she's hungry for now is fresh air.

She pushes the cart toward the checkout line. There's only one cashier serving the short line of customers with last-minute holiday purchases—bottles of wine, flowers, a pie. As she moves through the produce section, she sees a man and a young girl walking toward the front doors. The man is laughing, resting one hand gently on top of the girl's head, playfully holding a paper bag from the bakery just out of her reach with the other.

She recognizes the laugh before she recognizes him. He's wearing a stocking hat pulled low over his ears and a coat that she's never seen before, a different coat than the one he had worn to her house last night—and worn again when he left her this morning, after he'd shared her bed.

Twenty-Eight

There is a door in the house of her memory that she has not opened in a long time. There is a sign on the door, and when she wanders close, she reads the sign, as if the sign reveals what is behind the door, rather than concealing it.

The sign on the door is a simple story. "It's what I wanted, it's what I chose, and everything went smoothly."

She rarely passes the door, only when wandering aimlessly through the halls of memory in sleep or idleness, or when the scent of blood or cinnamon (*why cinnamon?*) pulls her there, straight to the closed door. When this happens, she reads the sign and passes by. Why bother opening the door? It's best left closed. The sign tells her what's inside, tells her all she needs to remember.

Twenty-Nine

She's driving straight somehow, but spinning, whirling, her body a tempest of nausea and elation. His lie had been a white lie, a *good* lie, an understandable, excusable lie. There was no other *woman*, no other love vying for his affections. He'd lied because he was waiting, no doubt, for the right time to tell her about his daughter.

Daughter. At that word something lurches inside her, something falls and sinks—or is it the nausea? She shakes her head, as if to clear it, to scatter any unwelcome thoughts rising up. The buzzing, pulsating energy has returned, and the whispers too, with more force.

We will be together. We will be together. Will—better than *must*, more confident, an incantation rather than a plea. The words rush through her, and she echoes them, murmuring them in assent. The delicious energy surges, expanding to absorb all her attention, swelling like the hum of cicadas; this is all she can feel and think, this invocation, this desire.

And then, like a sharp bell, like a lash, a different string of words cuts through the whirring, dizzying, throbbing hum—

What will this child be?

She resists the words, which have pierced her attention; she squirms like a moth on a pin.

Where had those words come from? Not from within, but without, from beyond—beyond herself, beyond even the invisible whirlwind that has captured her and carries her along. They had entered through the storm, entered *her*, leaving a long, unsettling silence in their wake.

Oh yes, she'd heard the words yesterday, during Mass. *What will this child be?*

She's just passing the church, she realizes; the church is two streets away, but directly parallel to where she is right now. A trick of the memory, then, a subconscious glitch.

Now's she passing the Outlaw, and her memory pivots there, to Adam, to the heat of his proximity. The cicada hum swells, the energy surges, the whispers return. *We will be together. We will be together.*

She gives herself over to them, as before, but not quite wholly. A splinter of her attention stays pinned, attuned to something below the fervor, something buried deep that has begun to stir.

The cloud cover is absolute, a dull, grayish white, the same color as the fields blurring by—there is no clear line between ground and sky, no horizon, as if she is no longer on earth at all, but inside some other, small, self-enclosed world; as if she could keep driving in a straight line and then eventually reappear where she'd begun, back at the stoplight at the entrance to town, caught in an endless loop. There is a heavy stillness in the air, no wind; the snow does not stir; it has hardened into a crust.

There is the house, appearing suddenly on the rise; as she approaches, she can see its face, the peaked ears, the windowed eyes, the porch railing teeth, eager, so eager to welcome her inside. It has been waiting, she realizes; all these years it's been waiting, biding its time, enduring other inhabitants, interlopers all, awaiting her return.

We will be together. We will be together. The house greets her as she punches her boots through the hardened snow and up the icy steps, her blue coat hanging open, her skin somehow immune to the cold, warmed by the buzzing, excitable energy coursing through her.

The front door is open! Not wide, just ajar, but still—how could she have neglected to shut the door? The cold has seeped into the house while she's been gone; even inside now, her breath hangs in a cloud around her face, visible. Better to keep on the coat, zip it up, close the front door securely, crank up the thermostat.

And then she notices. All the other doors, the *interior* doors, are closed. Every single one.

She pushes through the swinging door into the kitchen, which sits quiet and empty, innocent. She fills the kettle with water, the cold getting to her now, not her face or her hands, which are still somehow flushed with heat, but from within, in the hollow of her being.

From where she's standing at the sink, she can see outside—there is a cutout in the wall that looks through the mudroom to the windows that face the jagged, distant mountains. She reflexively looks for them, but they have vanished, erased by the impenetrable gray.

A flash of movement catches her eye; there's someone outside, no, *two* people; she can hear voices now, exchanging heated, unintelligible words. They are close to the house, just outside the mudroom door. She ventures closer, stooping to avoid the windows, crouching down, pressing her ear to the cold, metallic door.

"Why didn't you tell me?" A male voice, familiar somehow, but she can't place it. He's angry, but it's a wounded anger, coming from a place of pain.

"It was my decision." A female. Her voice is quiet, deadpan.

"I don't believe you."

A shriek, shrill and terrible, pierces the air. Simone jumps, cries out, claps her hands over her mouth before recognizing the sound. The kettle!

"Dammit," she mutters and hurries back into the kitchen, lifting the kettle from the red-hot rings so hastily that water spits out, sizzling on the hot stove.

She looks anxiously toward the mudroom door, alert for any sound—they had to have heard her—but nothing. After a moment she approaches the mudroom door and flings it open before she can change her mind, prepared for some kind of confrontation, or perhaps just the sight of two people fleeing through the snow—but there is no one there.

She glances down at the ground. The snow around the steps and all along the side of the house, as far out as she can see, is pristine—a brittle, crystalloid sheet, untouched. No human has stood or walked there for weeks.

She retreats back inside, shuts the door, locks it. She walks back into the kitchen, her mind revolving like a record that keeps spinning after the music has stopped. She can't quite catch it, can't quite get it to track a single thought.

"How could you let this happen?"

Cynthia? Her mother's voice, loud and clear, unmistakable, coming from somewhere beyond the kitchen.

She rushes through the chef's door, pushing it forcefully with both hands, calling out, "Cynthia?" Then, the word catching a bit in her throat, "Mother?"

Her voice echoes through the empty house, unanswered.

She approaches the closed door of her mother's room, feeling a sense of heaviness, dread, her feet like dragging stones.

There are voices behind the door, two of them, one sharp and interrogating, the other barely audible, a murmur.

"Don't blame *me*. I told you how to protect yourself. After everything I've done, everything I've taught you..."

"I know." Simone mouths the words even as she hears them, feels the molten shame ooze through her like lava. There is a long silence behind the closed door.

"Next week will be best. I can't do it this week. I have too much going on." The louder voice has lost its edge, becoming businesslike, resolved. "You'll only lose a week of school at most. And it's almost the holidays. No one will notice. We'll say you have the flu. It's bad this year. And waiting a week won't make a difference, not at this stage."

Almost the holidays. Simone closes her eyes and breathes in deeply, inhaling the scent of fresh pine and cinnamon, knowing that if she turns around, she will see a tall, barren evergreen against the bend of the staircase, securely set but awaiting decorations, silently witnessing this exchange behind the door, witnessing also the revelation that had occurred earlier that long-ago day, after these two creatures had broken its winter slumber with a saw blade, felling it only to raise it again, propped in a red metal stand, erect but disconnected from the earth.

It was after they brought home the tree ... that annual ritual, foraging in the mountain forest for a solitary pine, cutting it down, strapping it to the roof rack, driving it home, pulling it inside—she can still hear it, the hushed sound of branches dragging through snow. The same every year—except *that* year she was carrying a double burden: one impossibly light, weightless, known but not yet felt; the other heavy as a corpse, the deadweight of a shameful secret. The one she could not bear to carry any longer. The other ...

"But it's your grandchild." As she hears the words, barely audible behind the closed door, she remembers how hard it had been to speak them, how they had tumbled like rocks from her mouth.

A loud *smack*, the sound of an open palm striking skin. Simone lifts her hand to her cheek in pain, her body remembering.

"*Shut up! Shut up!*" The words are not shouted but seethed.

The kettle again, shrill and insistent, pulls her attention back to the kitchen. She rushes toward the sound without thinking, without registering that she had left the kettle in the center of the stove after turning off the burner, yet here it is, boiling again. She pushes the door, palms up, but it won't move. There is no lock on this door, not even a latch, but somehow it refuses her.

"You'll take this first." The voices are in the kitchen now. "Then in a few hours you'll take these. Well, you'll actually insert them, like a tampon." So calm, so matter-of-fact, professional, her mother in doctor mode. "Millions of women have done this. There is nothing to fear. These medications are totally safe. Safe and effective."

The sensation of a hand on her head, running gently down her hair, resting on her back, the warm glow of a steaming mug between her hands, cinnamon tea.

Simone presses her shoulder into the kitchen door, pushing her weight against it, impelled by an urge to see that girl again, to look into her eyes, to remember what she had felt in that moment, what she had wanted.

But when the door gives way, so suddenly she stumbles into the room, the kettle is cold and quiet on the counter; the chairs at the kitchen table sit empty and askew.

Thirty

She fills the bath right up to the edge of the overflow drain, so close that some water ripples in, gurgling down the pipe, the loudest sound she has heard in the past hour. Since the last—what should she call it: vision? hallucination? memory?—the house has been eerily quiet, not a peaceful quiet, but an anticipatory one, like the end of *The Iliad*, when both sides cease fighting for twelve days so the Trojans can mourn Hector, burn away his body and bury his bones, knowing all the while that war will resume.

How brutal, that poem. The unending spiral of violence, that cyclical doom. "Is Homer pro-war or anti-war?" She used to ask her students this, a trick question. War, for Homer, was an awful but inevitable reality, as much the stage of human drama as the earth itself. Violence begetting violence, doomed to repeat.

She eases her body into the water, melts into it, feeling the eerie echo of déjà vu. Is this what she had done last time? After the cinnamon tea? A vague flash of Cynthia sitting behind her, cross-legged on the toilet, monitoring, making sure she doesn't run.

But why would I run?

She tries to turn her attention toward Adam, not Adam *then* but Adam *now*—his face, his touch. She tries to conjure images, sensations from their night together, but the only image that surfaces is the one from earlier that day: Adam with his daughter.

A thought strikes, quick like an arrow, before she can twist away from it: Adam's daughter—that little girl had a half-sibling that Simone herself had carried once, carried and then extinguished.

Another thought, a second arrow: The life inside her now is the half-sibling of the life she'd carried then.

What will this child be?

This last thought is not an arrow; it does not penetrate her; it hovers in the distance, at the edge of her perception, like far-off but approaching thunder.

She sinks into the water, submerging herself fully, closing her eyes and mouth as if to keep all the voices and thought-arrows at bay, muffling her ears with water. *That is all hypothetical nonsense*, she tries to reassure herself. A murky world of *almost* and *could have* and *might have been*. The *now* is what matters, and right now, she just needs to follow the plan.

But underneath this resolve, which is brittle and thin, is a gathering tempest of doubt. Did she choose well then? Is she choosing well now?

When she thinks about that time, the facts are laid bare, but the memory of her inner world is hidden, as if her own past had happened to someone else, and she retains only the gist. The gist is neutral, mundane, perhaps even positive. (Cynthia had insisted it was positive—"Everything went well; you're back to baseline.") For her part, she has always regarded the event as an unpleasant but brief and *minor* episode from her past. A choice that was the obvious choice, a correction to a youthful indiscretion. *It hasn't affected me.*

And here she is faced with a parallel choice, but in a way its inverse: The first choice had created distance from Adam; it had been the beginning of the end—but this choice would bring them together, undoing somehow the first. And then they could begin, really begin, again, her womb like a fresh slate that could, perhaps, be written on sometime in the future, when she's truly ready, when the timing is right.

She breaks through the surface of the water and inhales sharply, deeply. How safe and enclosed she'd felt for a moment, embraced by the warm water, sheltered from the outside world. If only she could stay there, suspended; if only she didn't have to breathe.

She waits in the silence, with a sense of dread, unsure what she is going to hear.

Nothing, at first. But as she relaxes, rehearsing again the reasons to move forward with the plan, to press ahead, she can feel the house begin to hum its approval, to slowly resume its whispers, quiet at first, then whirring, purring like an oiled machine.

We will be together. We will be together.

And there's something else, some other sound—she sits up taller in the bath, turning her ear toward the door, pointing her attention toward—what is it? Laughter? A musical kind of laugh, light and airy and feminine and warm. She wonders at first if this is another echo of Cynthia, some intruding memory—but no, Cynthia never laughed like that. Cynthia could be comforting, in her own way, but she was rarely *warm*. She could be approving, but she never expressed *delight*. She was comforting in the way that a clean, well-ordered desk is comforting. But this—this is a sound like honey, like warm water, like falling into longed-for sleep. It is like the bath itself, soothing and subduing, and she relaxes into it, feeling her body go slack, letting the sound and the water carry her along to a place of acquiescence. The conflict in her chest, the storm of chariots and stallions, is quelled, the horses no longer pulling against her but grazing softly as the reins go slack.

She climbs out of the bath when the water turns tepid. And as she does, as her wet skin freezes in the chilled air, her muscles activating, tightening, the laughing gets louder, or perhaps closer, lulling her back into torpor.

All shall be well, says the laughing, sighing, soothing voice. *Do not be afraid*.

She's swathed herself in a double cocoon, a bathrobe under her long blue coat. She's walking out the bathroom door and into the front room, which is dancing with light. Light from where? Not the dull, shrouded sky; not the dim artificial lights.

From there!—on the stairs, the shimmering pillar of jeweled color, rippling and pulsing, its diamond eyes flashing, projecting beams of light across the room.

Let it be, says the voice, the honeyed voice, still rippling with delight, which Simone realizes is coming from the apparition; mouthless, yet somehow it speaks.

Be it done, says the voice, the prismatic eyes whirling, fixed on her, holding her in their light. *Be it done. Thy will.*

The apparition moves backward, never breaking its gaze, and Simone follows mutely, entranced. How lucky she is! To be visited in this way, to have something so beautiful and numinous break into her world, to be chosen!

As she passes the French doors into the living room, she sees something in her periphery, a figure on the couch, curled up as if in pain. She moves toward the door, wanting a closer look, but as she turns, the apparition is suddenly in front of her, blocking her way—somehow it has flashed instantly across the room, its eyes dark and red, like pools of blood, losing for a moment their luminescence.

Startled, she looks back toward the stairs, to where the apparition had just been—and there it is again! Jeweled eyes spinning light, a whirlwind of blurring, dancing color coaxing her upward.

The voice is somehow behind her now, curling around her shoulders like a tentacle of air, brushing itself against her cheek, a caress.

My eyes see all, my eyes bless all. I reject nothing. I judge no one. I welcome all. Night is as day.

"Night is as day," Simone echoes aloud, her words entwining with the voice, her breath with its vapor.

Together, one following the other, they approach the door of her bedroom. Of course this is where they have been going; she's known all along, noticed how all the doors in the house are closed, all except this one, which hangs open, as if inhaling, and is not dark inside but lit from within, with that same rosy-orange light the apparition is casting all over the walls. She knows that the vision is escorting her, accompanying her to complete her task; she'd set up everything in the inner chamber before her bath, when her hands were still quivering with indecision, lining up the packets and pills on her bedside table, next to a glass of water and a book—there will be an interval between taking the medicine and the completion, time to kill.

When they reach the door, something happens. As the apparition crosses the threshold, watching her with its dazzling column of mirrored eyes, the vision flickers for a moment, turning gray and indistinct; the whole room darkens, passing into shadow; the light from the eyes abruptly cuts off—but only for the briefest instant. Then, like a blurred image snapping into focus, the light and color and form of the vision return; the voice and its vapor curl against her ear once more, offering comfort, support.

But in that instant, that stretched-out second of shadow, she had heard something, she was certain—not the soothing voice or the humming house, but a groan, a deep cry of despair. She pauses, listening, searching, trying to hear past the voice that continues to murmur its approval and delight in her ear.

They've entered the bedroom now, the outer room; the apparition sways and sashays toward the inward chamber, but then it happens again: The room darkens, the vision disperses like smoke, and the voice in her ear turns raspy and hollow, desiccating into a dry, grating whisper—and behind it, close by, she can hear someone sobbing.

When the apparition returns, snapping back into form and color, her senses recoil, overpowered; the swirling eyes and their radiations are no longer dazzling but blinding—there had been something reorienting, grounding, something *true* in the brief tenebrosity.

On an impulse, she steps backward, away from the vision, away from the inner room—the apparition, moving toward her, dissipates, then reassembles. She knows where the cry is coming from now, from behind her, from the closet.

She turns toward the closet—but the apparition is there, blocking her path, churning and pulsating, eyes ablaze.

I want what's best for you. The honeyed voice, maternal and kind, echoing words Cynthia had said to her, but with such tenderness. *Behind that door is only pain.*

From the inner room now, a new sound—two voices talking in hushed, intimate tones, laughing quietly, exchanging lavish promises.

"No matter what happens," he says, "we will be together."

The words hook her heart, plunging deep, pulling her forward; she rushes into a small room brimming with morning sun, and there by the window is the face of a boy she once knew, his eyes alight with the flush of first love. Yet looking at him again, after all this time, she realizes he no longer exists; he has been swallowed by time, both he and the girl who loved him, and the years between that morning and right now have merged into a river, a great chasm, as unbridgeable as the river Styx.

The room cuts to shadow; she turns to see a dissipating cloud of smoke and a veiled form emerging from within, a flash of a cadaverous face—then the apparition regathers, flicks back into color. And in this instant she recognizes a pattern.

Always in that same spot—the middle of the outer room—the apparition crosses some kind of invisible trip wire and dissolves into smoke and shadow. There, and also at the doorway from the hall. Why would that be?

Her curiosity has awakened, a hungry rat. She crouches to her hands and knees, waving her hand in space, feeling nothing, then peering down at the well-lit floorboards. *What's that?*

Across the gleaming boards, she can see a jagged line of scattered particles, which she first mistakes for sand before remembering: the exorcized salt. Very powerful, the priest had said. And she had dutifully, madly, sprinkled it across every doorway in the house, until finally, in this room, the last room, dispensing the few remaining grains in a haphazard streak across the floor.

Thirty-One

Quick, now: the unmasking.

The seduction has been slow, playing painfully on her fears and desires, but this—this part happens swiftly.

Still on the floor, on her knees, she lunges forward and scatters the salt across the floor, whisking her hands rapidly so the grains fly everywhere—can even one grain hold some kind of power? She can't believe this is true, but she trusts it anyway, assumes that dispersing the salt over the entire floor will disrupt the vision for good and reveal its true nature, which she has already begun to understand.

Before the vision dissipates, one final time, the undulating pillar of jeweled eyes, for an instant, solidifies enough for her to see and understand its shape—not a pillar, or column, or whirlwind, but a *snake*, the bulbous, hooded head, the thick body rising up in strike pose, the long tail coiling, dragging behind. And the dazzling, glinting orbs, in this last glimpse, are less like eyes than *mouths*, red and ripe and open.

The serpent lunges toward her, orifices gaping, each one flicking with a forked, wet tongue, with fangs like shards of glass. She covers her face in terror, waiting for the strike—but nothing comes. She looks up in time to see a column of smoke rush toward her and disappear.

The room drains instantly of light and color; only weak, shrouded sunlight seeps into the room, which is arrayed in degrees of shadow, from dark to dim, depending upon proximity to the windows, the only sources of dull light.

Except ... one foot away from her, right where the apparition had been, is a moving silhouette, a three-dimensional shadow, a figure made visible only by the total lack of light—it is like a cutout in the fabric of reality, pure absence. And yet it moves and somehow speaks, in a voice devoid of warmth, inhuman, a death rattle of words.

This is where you first came to me, in the quiet and the dark.

She can hear the sobs clearly now, the moans of agony—they are coming from behind the closet door. The one door in the house that she has not yet opened.

And yet, to move toward the closet means moving toward the shadow-being—already she can feel its darkness pull at her like gravity. She is not sure she has the strength to resist it, move past it. Her body feels like ballast, unresponsive to her will.

This is where you first came to me.

This is where you belong.

This heaviness, this weight, this sense of dreadful inevitability—it is a feeling she *knows*, one that has haunted her, shadowed her for years. She has even named it—*the undertow*—though she is able to banish it for the most part through hyperactivity and overwork, so that it only finds her, claims her, in unguarded moments, most often in the borderland between wakefulness and sleep. It is a weight, an unbearable weight, not of grief, but of something futile and unending: despair.

Then—in the distance, the deep distance, the far distance, she can hear a rumbling. Thunder, she thinks at first—but no, no, not in winter. Perhaps an earthquake. Her mind cycles through impossible possibilities. A volcanic eruption. An approaching army, arrayed for battle, the earth trembling beneath thousands of marching feet.

She closes her eyes, attending to this distant sound as a way of shielding herself from the droning, hissing words that swarm around her ears like insects.

We made a pact that night. Sealed in blood.

She cannot hear so much as *feel* the rumbling, the quaking—it is approaching from beyond, from outside, yet its force reverberates into her, down through the hollow beneath her heart.

Something is happening; something is stirring, down in the deep, dark well.

Don't fight. Accept.

Does it know? Can it hear? Is it—afraid?

We will be together. We must.

Words hissed as a threat. Not as fate.

She's moving now, her limbs responsive enough to bend, support her weight, as she crawls across the floor, toward the black hole in the center of the room, whose contours have begun to morph and shift, oscillating between the shape of a shrouded woman and the form of a hooded snake.

The whole house is quaking now, the windows rattling, the floorboards creaking and groaning from intense pressure. Is this another one of its tricks? To keep her from opening the door?

But no—as the quaking intensifies, the shadow seems to be shrinking, caving in on itself, like a dark star in gravitational collapse. It has no discernible shape, no clear form whatsoever now; it is a black gash, a vanishing stain.

Nothing left but the voice now, which has diminished to a thin rasp, barely audible amid the roar and clash of the army closing in.

Don't open . . .

But her hand is on the knob, she is no longer listening; she is twisting to open a door closed long ago, closed and locked and sealed.

At her touch, it opens easily. She flings it wide.

Inside is the girl, the girl she once was, huddled in the corner in a puddle of her own blood. She looks at her, and the veil is lifted from her memory of that night and she remembers the pain, all of it, the coiling within her, as if her body was fighting back, struggling against what she'd done—then the awful release, the rush of clotted blood, and the sense of relief, followed quickly by a cavernous grief, feeling hollowed out, emptied. She had fled and hid, after seeing the tiny orb floating in the water, the silent messenger; she had hid from her mother to grieve and bleed alone, and hours later, her mother found her, leading her wordlessly from the closet and back to bed, a silent pact passing between them never to speak of this, to erase it from memory, to layer this moment with a soft, simple story of a meaningless, harmless act, a *sensible* act, a *good* act, an act best forgotten. And so the memory—the terrible complexity of pain, sorrow, relief, and fear—had rolled up like a scroll, so much concealed within, but only a simple sentence on the surface, easily accessible: *I had an abortion, a long time ago, and it was no big deal.*

This time, the voice in her ear is Cynthia's: *We did the right thing.*

One word: bellowing up from the depths, rushing up like something long imprisoned, able to break free because what has been contorted and conflicted within her is suddenly, forcefully *aligned*.

There she comes, that long-buried oracle, that divine echo, climbing up out of her well: Truth, naked and unveiled, beautiful and terrible, climbing up out of her well. Surfacing to help Simone say the truest word she's ever spoken.

No.

With this word, whetted and fierce, she shatters the lie, that locked door of a lie that has so long concealed the source of her nameless pain, her great wound.

She can hear the house protesting, groaning, wood splitting apart, doors flying open, the shattering of glass. Whatever has been coming is upon them now—the earthquake, the apocalyptic dawn, the armed hosts with terrible trumpets that agitate the ground.

She bends to embrace the girl, opening her coat to envelop them both; they are together now, huddled in the corner, waiting for the world to stop reeling, to right itself, and as Simone looks down at her trembling body, she feels herself begin to bleed.

Thirty-Two

When she awakens, she has no idea how much time has passed, no idea, at first, where she is, sitting alone in the quiet dark. Then it returns, the memory of the impossible things that happened, a great flood of images like a fireworks show, and then, nothing. Stillness.

She is sitting, legs splayed, on the hardwood floor of her closet, which is empty. There is no one else there, no phantom of her former self, no shape-shifting chimera; the house is silent and still. The door to the closet is open, letting in some dim light, too dim for daylight. Moonlight. Soft streaks across the floor, across her lower body, which she explores gently with her hands, expecting her fingers to come back sticky with blood, but they are clean and dry. She is clean and dry, her body whole.

She is startled at the relief that floods her body, like a great rush of water, from the crown of her head to her toes, all bare. "Thank God," she whispers. "Thank God." She is shocked at how easily the words spring to her lips, how sincerely she means them, how grateful she is to realize that the being in her womb, the quickening orb, is still safely enshrined in her body, still whirring, unfurling within her.

What will this child be?

She welcomes the question now. She is open to the mystery.

She rises unsteadily to her feet, like a foal testing its limbs for the first time, newly born yet somehow already standing. She lowers her head to duck through the narrow door and steps out into the room.

Night has fallen. Or rather, night has sprung, night has appeared, bearing gifts. The windows glow with a deep yet radiant blue; the night is somehow more luminous than the empty darkness inside the house.

Yes, empty. For the first time since she arrived, the house feels blank, inert, ordinary—no longer watching, no longer urging; its hungry vigilance is gone. And yet she still feels the quiet presence of someone's attention.

The air in the room is frigid, but with an invigorating, cleansing cold; she feels awake and alert, her eyes open. The air is stirring; there's a cold breeze, not coming through the windows, which are closed, but through the door to the bedroom, which is open wide—and not just this door, she sees as she walks into the hall and looks down below: all the doors. Every door in the house is open.

Somehow this is not frightening; she does not feel exposed or vulnerable or invaded—no, the opposite. Something has been driven out; something has been banished.

She walks down the stairs slowly, her blue coat open and trailing behind her, making a soft hushing sound against the stairs. She slips on her boots, which she'd left by the front door, and walks through the open door into the night.

The sky above her is a deep blue canopy; the clouds have been rolled back; all she can see are stars, streaks and swirls and luminous patterns, a dazzling tangle of stars, each one letting through a secret hidden light.

She crosses the porch and descends the steps into the front yard. She walks past the lone, watchful tree so she can look up at the sky unobscured, her feet sinking deep into the snow.

There, straight ahead, emerging from the horizon, is the white-gold moon, full and whole and radiant, somehow not competing with the starlight, as if the same light flows through the one to the others.

And the snow! Newly fallen and stretching out before her like infinity, echoing the soft radiance of the moon in a silent call-and-response. The snow, like the house, seems changed, altered; it is no longer hiding the earth but adorning it; not obscuring but reflecting, revealing.

On a whim, she lowers herself down into it, sinks back into the soft whiteness, her blue coat spread beneath her like a blanket. She can feel the chilled, velvety touch of the fresh powder against her hair, the tips of her ears, and she welcomes the cold, the clarifying cold. She is unsure how long she'll be able to endure it, stretched out under the dome of the sky, but more than anything right now, more than warmth or sleep or comfort—more than anything, she wants to see.

She whispers the words, which billow in a cloud around her face.

"I want to see."

It begins with one star among the rest, a pinprick of white light that appears to be moving. Not arcing like a meteorite, but expanding outward, opening up, dilating into a large, luminous globe.

A form emerges against the sky, within the orb: a woman—it's her, the woman from the icon in the alcove, Our Lady of the Sign. But that icon is a mere shadow of what she is seeing now, only a static portrayal of something that is moving and alive. The woman raises her arms, palms out, and the red blur of her heart blooms into another circle, not an opaque orb, but a portal, a door.

Within this circle Simone sees a cacophonous blur of flickering shapes, broken images, scattered and discordant. She watches as each image spins out into a sphere, spheres gathered up into an annular ring around the woman, just like the icon with its array of human faces. But instead of hooded saints and biblical hybrids, she sees—could it be?

Her mother. Simone sees her, perhaps clearly for the first time: the lonely woman she has become and, there, in an opening on her breast, hidden in her heart, the scared, abandoned girl she once was. She sees the wounded girl in the heart of her mother, a woman born of pain and fear, and she watches as that image is taken up into the sign, into one of the whirling wheels.

And who is this, in another orbiting sphere, is it ... herself? She is one of the broken images, bearing on her chest the form of a huddled girl within, the girl who hid and wept and bled alone on the closet floor.

She sees it all: her own pain, the girl she was; her mother's pain, the girl she was; the women they are, the women they will be; the child who was lost, the child burgeoning in her now; the mother *she will be*; their broken, limping motherhood, her mother's and her own, taken up, somehow, by the lady of the sign, into the gaping *yes* of her heart, that opening through which some greater light—she can see it now, streaks of a fiery dawn—will come.

The vision dissolves as quickly as it unfolded, shapes and colors rushing inward, collapsing back into the compact light of a single bright star. Her gaze lingers on where it had been, searching the ghostly trail of the Milky Way overhead; she is already unsure of what she has witnessed, even as the afterimage still plays across her vision, imprinted on everything she sees.

Flecks of white spin toward her, and for a moment she thinks it is beginning again—but when they alight on her lips with a soft, cold kiss, she realizes: It has begun to snow.

Thirty-Three

She makes one stop on her way out of town. She had planned for none, planned to leave swiftly, face set toward the ring of mountains to the north and a road going toward them that would carry her up and out of this valley for the last time. She is not frantic; she is unafraid; she is curiously, eerily calm, as calm as the hushed, pristine night around her, as calm as the quiet snow.

But as she drives down Main Street, one last pass through the town's deserted center, she sees his truck, parked outside the Outlaw. No sign of him; the bar is dark and silent, like every other building on the street, closed up tight. It's Christmas morning, she realizes, still the predawn dark, hours from sunlight, but Christmas nonetheless. *Why is his truck parked here? Why isn't he home with his daughter?* Perhaps he had only the day with her, and now he is alone, stumbling home after too many whiskeys, avoiding as long as he could the echo of a lonely house. He is in his own battle, she realizes; what they had sought in each other, sought and found, was temporary solace, a distraction to dull the sharp edges of a complicated, cracked-up life. He could not save her, nor she him. She cannot even save herself. But maybe she can leave something for him, some sense of closure, a few sincere words. Perhaps whatever has come for her this night, bent down to her in rescue, will come for him someday too.

She pulls to a stop behind his truck, fumbles for a scrap of paper, a pen, writing down the words that come. When she steps out of the car, her heavy boots anchor her to the ground, steady and sure. She shivers in the subzero air; she left the long blue coat hanging in the closet, an empty cocoon—foolish, perhaps, but somehow fitting. She won't need it now.

She walks quickly over to his windshield, the wipers already frozen against the glass. She pulls one free, rolling her note into a tight scroll and tucking it safely underneath, after reading the words one last time.

> *Adam,*
> *I saw you with your daughter. She's beautiful.*
> *Let's choose what we've chosen.*
>   *—S.*

Away from the town, away from the last glimmers of artificial light, she climbs up, ascending toward a sky that is cracked open, like a split geode crowded with stars, more stars than she's ever seen, than she's ever imagined seeing. Though she'd lived here once, in this place, and has driven this same pass a hundred times, somehow she never noticed; she never truly *saw*.

One thing left to do. It is an hour earlier there, but still the middle of the night. She will wake him. She wants to wake him. Now she has become the messenger; she is the one bearing news.

The phone rings only twice before she hears his voice—warm and eager, but tinged with worry. He says her name as a question, and she knows what he's asking. Not who is calling, but where has she been? Where is she going now? Is she moving toward him or away?—she has misjudged, she realizes, how much he would miss her.

"I'm coming home," she says, "and I have something to tell you."

She's cresting the long hill now, and the road begins to level, straightening out. The gap behind her that opens to the valley is narrowing, closing, the last visible lights of Fall River swallowed, one by one, by the night.

"Okay," he says. He is hesitant, unsure. "Good news I hope?"

"Yes." The word rises easily from within her, up from under her heart. She says it again. "Yes, I promise. Yes."

The dark pines line the road like sentinels, watching over silently as she passes through, their tops like arrows pointed toward the stars, which seem somehow to be streaming down to her, tiny messengers each bearing a light that she's only just learning how to see.